HALF THE
BATTLE

HALF THE BATTLE

Lynn Hall

CHARLES SCRIBNER'S SONS | New York

Copyright © 1982 Lynn Hall
Library of Congress Cataloging in Publication Data
Hall, Lynn.   Half the battle.
Summary: Jealous of the attention that has
always been focused on his blind brother, Loren
takes drastic action to achieve recognition for
himself when the teenagers enter an endurance
ride on horseback.
[1. Brothers and sisters—Fiction.
2. Blind—Fiction.   3. Physically handicapped—
Fiction.   4. Horses—Fiction]   I. Title.
PZ7.H1458Hal   [Fic]   81-23285
ISBN 0-684-17348-4   AACR2

1 3 5 7 9 11 13 15 17 19 F/C 20 18 16 14 12 10 8 6 4 2

Printed in the United States of America

HALF THE
BATTLE

Chapter 1

The town of Rebano seemed to lean back against the Sangre de Christo mountains. Desert winds from the lowlands to the east periodically sandblasted Rebano, shaping trees and small buildings into a westward cant.

Between sandstorms the grassy plateau that held Rebano was one of the prettiest stretches of farmland in northern New Mexico. The small highway that bisected it was just busy enough to bring a smattering of tourist trade but too small to have sprouted many billboards. Travelers had an uncluttered view of rolling grasslands, cottonwood trees spreading their shade over small flocks of sheep, the sheltering circle of gray-green mountains, and a brilliant turquoise sky.

At the edge of town, just off the highway, stood the Rebano Consolidated School. The central building was old, sandstone, a mother hen to the modern brick wings angling away from it.

This afternoon, as on every Friday afternoon, a dusty tan compact car with an Area Education Agency sticker on the door sped across the plateau at just ten miles over the speed limit, slowed abruptly at the city limits, and coasted into the school parking lot. Anita Blanco unfolded herself out of the car, gathered an armload of oversized books, and made a token swat at the road dust on her clothes.

Blair Liskey waited until the hallway traffic noises disappeared and the sounds of last-hour classes began in the rooms around him. In the faintly echoing hallway stillness he began making his way toward the little office just off the learning center. He knew the way perfectly well, and only trailed his fingertips along the surface of the lockers out of habit.

Before him was darkness, except for a small round area immediately ahead in which he could see light and a blur of distorted shapes. The shadowy mass to his right was a portion of the locker wall, the brighter area was the learning center, which he knew to be a large round room, brightly lit and crisscrossed with bookshelves.

He was a tall boy, still somewhat narrow through the shoulders but round faced, with just a suggestion of extra flesh above his Levis. His hair was a mass of dark curls, his skin clear and fresh. His lips were sensuously full, and figured prominently in the imaginings of several Rebano High School girls.

As Blair made his way down the long hallway he sensed the Friday afternoon electricity in the air. For him, of course, the day meant Mrs. Blanco, but the sense of release was there for everybody, students and teachers equally. He could hear it in the lift of a teacher's voice, in the jokes of the cafeteria women. He heard the library aide in the learning center humming under her breath, so softly that no one but Blair Liskey caught it.

When the linoleum of the hallway floor changed to learning center carpet beneath his shoes, Blair veered left two and a half strides and swung into the little wedge-shaped office that was his and Mrs. Blanco's on Friday afternoons. She was there already. He felt her warmth and heard her soft rustlings even before he centered the blurred mass that was her in his tiny field of vision.

"Hi, gorgeous." He located his chair and dropped into it.

"Blair," she said, and the sandpaper quality of her voice delighted him, as it had for years.

"How's it going?" she said. "Any problems you want to talk about?"

He shrugged. It had been a routine week. He couldn't find anything in his memory that could be used now, to bring her close, to ignite the caressing warmth her voice had held for him once or twice, a long time ago . . .

"Going okay, I guess. I'll miss you, over summer vacation."

"I'll miss you, too." Her voice was brisk, but Blair heard the smile in it.

Before he could answer, Mrs. Blanco went on. "I don't think you'll need me next year, Blair. You'll be a senior, you've been in this building three years now, and you know how to work the visual aid equipment better than I do. So I think—"

"No! I mean, I still need to see you. You're about the only friend I've got. Just talking to you, I really need that. You're the only one who understands what I'm going through."

"Bull ticky," she said flatly. "If I'm the only friend you've managed to make in this school, after all these years, then that's a pretty poor commentary on your personality, isn't it?"

Fall back and regroup, he thought wryly. Something inside him rose to the excitement of doing verbal battle with this woman, this one person in his world who knew him for what he was, and liked him anyway.

"I didn't mean my only friend, exactly. But most of the guys are into some sport or other . . ." He let his words drift in the air. No self-pity in his tone. That didn't work with Mrs. B.

She laughed suddenly, a big, warm, natural laugh that made Blair's lips twitch upward in spite of himself.

"Blair Liskey, what are we going to do with you? I think maybe a career in law or politics, where your powers of persuasion could make you rich. Don't give me that junk about the other boys being out for sports. You're going to out-sport them all, this summer, aren't you?"

"Oh. You read that article in the paper."

"Yes, and I think it's a fine idea. You're getting a little pudgy around the middle. A good hundred-mile endurance ride might turn a little of that flab into muscle. I suppose a thing like that involves a lot of training. Preparation. Like running a marathon?"

Blair nodded. "Yeah. Loren and I will start working the horses as soon as school lets out. It takes a lot of know-how to get the horses hardened right. And the ride itself is tough, and dangerous. Even for a sighted person," he added, because she didn't seem sufficiently impressed.

"Yes, I'm sure. It's a good thing you have Loren, isn't it?"

Blair's face hardened for an instant. Mrs. Blanco saw, and said, "Have you decided yet about college? You'll have

4

to start making some decisions along those lines before too long, you know."

He looked away toward the wall. He was unaware of the action, but Mrs. Blanco knew it, knew he was hiding from her.

"I don't want to go to college."

"What do you want to do," she asked calmly, "sell pencils on a street corner?"

"How about Navajo craft on a highway corner?" he countered, trying to grin. "Is that in the same category?"

"I don't know, is it? You tell me. Is it what you really want to do with your life, or is it an easy out?"

"I don't know." He turned away from her again. The day had soured. Who was this woman, anyway, to tell him how to run his life. She didn't have to go groping around every day of her life, being the blind kid, the one everybody felt sorry for. Hell with her.

He stood up. "Well, I guess I'm taking up your time, from the more deserving blindies."

Mrs. Blanco stood, too. Her voice betrayed no reaction to his sarcasm. "I do have to talk to Kim awhile, this afternoon. Not more deserving, no, Blair. Just newer to all this, and a little more in need of me than you are."

She picked up his hand and held it for an instant. "All my kids are special to me, Blair, and especially you because we've known each other for so long. I've watched you grow from a scared little fifth grader into a fine young man, and I have no doubt at all that you're going to succeed in life. And if I'm not seeing you anymore as your visual aid specialist, it's not because I've rejected you in any way, it's because you've outgrown your need for that kind of help. Okay?"

5

He mumbled something and left the office, bumping into Kim Cramer, who was waiting her turn. Her armload of cumbersome large-print textbooks banged to the floor.

"Sorry," he said grudgingly as he kneeled and groped for the books. He didn't feel like being polite. He didn't know Kim, but he disliked the idea of her, of her blindness—of her being blind in his high school.

There was still a half hour before school was out. Blair stood near the learning center's big central desk and moved his head slowly from side to side, looking for motion that might be the library aide. She appeared as a voice near his elbow.

"Can I get you something, Blair?"

"Yeah, Jenny, I was working on *The Catcher in the Rye* last week, for my book report, remember? You said you'd hold it for me."

"Here t'is, with your place still marked. You need any help with the machine, you just call me, okay?"

He nodded and made his way to the closed-circuit television in a far corner of the room behind a jutting bookshelf. He sat before the machine and slid the opened book onto the surface before him, but didn't turn the machine on. He felt deflated by Mrs. Blanco, as though she had failed to come through for him, somehow. A hundred-mile endurance ride, on horseback, over rugged mountain country, in two days. That was something for anybody to accomplish. But for a blind guy to have the guts to tackle it, that deserved a little more than just, "Be good exercise for you, Blair, you're getting fat." And to say he didn't need her anymore. That wasn't true.

The small boy inside him wanted to cry, wanted to

crawl close to Mrs. Blanco and burrow into her warmth, feel her arms around him, her hand stroking his hair. Like that time when he was first mainstreamed into the public school after five years in the security of the state school for the blind, and found out that he would have to repeat fifth grade because of the adjustment. Found out he would be in the same class as Loren. Found out he was alone in his dark world while everyone around him pushed so fast in the hall. And once he hadn't been able to find the boys' restroom in time. Mrs. Blanco was there to hold him and soothe him, and joke him into a smile.

But now he was too old. Too big for cuddling. Then why didn't the *need* go away?

He heard the squeak of Jenny's shoes behind him, smelled the approach of her hand lotion. Swiftly his foot moved out, found the cord to the video machine, and pulled.

"Need some help over here, Blair?"

"I can't seem to get it turned on." He flipped the on-switch several times, while his senses opened toward her woman-warmth, her caring.

"Hmm, that's funny. Let me see." Her arm brushed him as she reached across to work the switches. Blair put his arm around her. She stepped back, sputtering with embarrassment.

With penitence in his voice he said, "I'm sorry. I didn't mean to get smart or anything. It's just that, I don't know, you've been so much help to me all year, and I feel like you're my friend, you know? And I don't have any way of knowing what you look like except by touch."

"Brown hair, hazel eyes, and too old for you," she snapped. "And here," she stooped and plugged in the

7

cord. "That was the trouble, it was just unplugged. Now you behave yourself."

He waited until she was gone before he allowed himself to grin. With renewed spirits he positioned his book and leaned toward the television screen before his face. One by one, the much-magnified words came into focus, and he entered the story.

The bell rang, ending the last class of the last day of the next-to-last week of school. Although the old raucously clanging bell had been replaced two years ago by a gentler chime, the effect was as it had always been, a stampede of released captives. Blair was the exception. He read on, another slow paragraph, another slow page, reluctant to leave the story and become himself again.

Finally, when the din of clanging locker doors and shouting voices began to lessen, he flipped off the machine and made his way to his locker.

"Lor?" he asked. No answer. Sighing, Blair leaned against the locker to wait. While it was fresh in his mind he began going over the plot line of *The Catcher in the Rye*, planning his synopsis and interpretation of author's motives for Monday's book report which, for Blair, would be verbal rather than written.

"Hey, Liskey, shift your bones, man." The voice belonged to Bob Red Hawk. Blair moved back away from Bob's locker door. He wasn't intimidated by the huge Navajo linebacker, but he didn't antagonize The Hawk, either.

"You seen my brother anywhere?" Blair asked.

"Out in the parking lot, man. I just saw him out there.

Hey, Liskey, was that the straight sheepdip, that story about you in the paper? About that hundred-mile ride? You ain't really going to do that, are you?"

"Sure I am. Why? Don't you think I can?"

"Don't get your bowels in an uproar, man. I never said nothing like that. Hey, I think it's great. I sure couldn't do it."

Blair glowed.

"Course, you probably couldn't do it either, if you didn't have Loren, right? Well, we got a scrimmage this aft, I better get out there. See ya, Liskey."

"See ya," Blair muttered, but the hall was already empty. As he made his way down the long hallway toward the door nearest the parking lot, his deflation at The Hawk's parting shot began to sour into resentment toward Loren, without whose wonderful help poor old Blair wouldn't be able to do a darned thing, not the Sangre Trek, not anything.

As he came down the outside steps he heard Loren call his name. "Where the hell were you?" he flared as he got into the pickup. "You were supposed to meet me at my locker."

"Sorry about that." Loren's voice was flippant. He kicked the old truck to life and maneuvered it out onto the highway.

"Sorry don't feed the bulldog," Blair muttered. "Next time, be where you're supposed to be."

Blair slid low in the seat and braced his knees against the dash. His book report was gone from his mind now; he was tuned entirely into the brother beside him and the vibrations coming from Loren were purely hostile. It

9

wasn't a new sensation for Blair, but Loren's hostility unerringly found Blair's vulnerability and damaged him. Right now he needed to be away from his brother, to savor The Hawk's words. "I think it's great. I sure couldn't do it." He needed to replay that tape in his mind until it drowned out the part about, "You couldn't do it without Loren."

He thought about the weeks to come, about the training he and Loren, Kade and Sundance, would be going through together and about the Sangre Trek shining like a trophy at the end of the training period. Am I going to survive it? he wondered. Eight weeks of riding every day with Loren, ten miles, twenty miles a day till the horses are muscled up. Steep mountain trails, river crossings, all that, and I'll be at Loren's mercy. And then the ride itself. A hundred miles in two days, fifty or sixty other people all racing each other on those narrow trails. Accidents. It's going to be tough, man. What made me think I could do it? What made me want to try?

He knew. It was Bob Red Hawk smelling of sweat after football practice, and Stretch Hernandez during basketball season, and Blair Liskey the blind kid who was only that and nothing more. One more year. Just one more year and it was going to be slam bam, so long ma'am. Today Mrs. Blanco shoves him out of her office, next year it will be Mom and Dad saying, move on, kid. You're on your own. Go out there and make it in the big world, we'll send you a Christmas card. Then, boy, Blair Liskey better be something more than the blind kid. There better be some guts inside there, somewhere.

Are there?

How the hell do I know? I've never had to *do* anything. The Trek . . .

Loren said, "That was some interview you gave the newspaper."

"What are you griping about now?"

"Oh nothing, mister wonderful. But you did manage to make the Trek sound like a solo effort. I didn't see too many mentions of good old baby brother who takes care of the horses twelve months of the year and who will be doing the ride too, and if I didn't, you couldn't."

Blair sat up. "Listen, I told the kid who interviewed me all about your part in it. If he didn't choose to print every word exactly like I told it to him, I can't help that. He probably thought it made a better story this way, you know, blind kid conquers mountain and all that stuff."

Loren snapped, "Well, I'll tell you one thing, hermano, when we start working those horses this summer, you're doing your half, you got that? I'll do Kade, but Sundance is your job, and if you and him can't keep up with Kade and me, that's tough luck."

"Don't worry, we'll keep up." Blair's jaw was rigid. When he felt the truck slow for the turnoff he said, "Drop me at the shop."

"You're there."

With relief that he knew was mutual, Blair got out of the truck and slammed the door. Gravel rained against his leg as the truck roared away.

The Navajo Shop was a little box of a building close to the highway. It was genuine adobe, with piñon beams over the door and windows. At one time it had been a tiny house, then a gas station, and, for the last six years, Norma Liskey's marginally profitable souvenir shop.

Inside, it was blessedly cool, thanks to the adobe walls and the broad blades of the ceiling fan. It smelled of wool

11

and leather and his mother's hair spray. Blair heard pages rustling.

"Howdee there, ma'am," Blair said. "Your sign says Navajo Shop and I'd like to buy me a Navajo. I'll take a princess model, about five-foot-seven, terrific body, blue eyes—"

"Blue eyes?" Norma Liskey laughed. "I'd have to special-order that model for you. Thousand dollar deposit, at least."

"Take it out of my clothes allowance." He cocked his head toward the soft fizz of an opened pop bottle on the glass-topped counter between them. "Can I have a shot of your pop?"

"It's about gone. Get yourself a new one." She handed him coins from her cash box. "I was just reading your interview in the *Register*. A very nice story, I thought. I'll have to get copies for Grandma and Grandpa, and maybe Aunt Ruby."

Under the front window was an old-fashioned chest-type Coke machine, with bottles suspended on tracks that converged at a release hatch. Blair pulled a bottle out of the third row, opened it, and took a long pull.

"This isn't Coke. It's Orange Crush." He grimaced and put the bottle down.

"Oh, sorry, hon. I must have loaded the machine wrong this morning."

He waited, but she didn't offer more money for another bottle. "But I can't stand Orange Crush." His voice sounded more petulant than he'd intended, but his whole mood was sour by now. First Mrs. Blanco, then The Hawk and Loren, and now not even Mom on his side. He felt bleak.

"Read me the newspaper story, would you?" he asked. "All I know about it is that Loren was steamed because he didn't get top billing."

He wasn't aware of the look Norma threw him. She cleared her throat. " 'Blair Liskey Plans Endurance Ride.' That's the headline. 'By Casey Lopez. When your roving reporter began asking junior class members about their plans for the summer, I got mostly boring answers, like helping out at home or working at the Taco Tree. But not so with Blair Liskey. The intrepid Blair is laying plans to compete in the Eighth Annual Sangre Trek, held every August here in our own hills. The Sangre Trek, Blair tells me, is a hundred-mile endurance ride to be completed in two days, on horseback. Approximately sixty riders from all over the country will start the ride, but only a few are expected to complete it.

" 'The winner will be the first rider to complete the ride with his horse in good enough physical condition to pass the final veterinary examination. The ride will demand expert conditioning for horse and rider, and top-notch athletic ability by both, since the ride will be held over rugged mountain trails.

" 'Competing in the Sangre Trek would be a big undertaking for any horseman, but for Blair, who has only three percent vision and is legally blind, this reporter considers it an act of genuine heroism. Blair will be accompanied on the ride by his brother Loren, also a junior.' "

Silence filled the little shop.

Finally Norma said, "I can see how Loren might have his nose a little out of joint. 'Accompanied by his brother Loren' isn't exactly giving him his just deserts, it it? After all, he'll be in charge of conditioning the horses, and Sun-

13

dance will follow Kade on the Trek—I'm not downplaying what you're doing," she said hastily. "It's just that I think Loren should get a little of the glory, too, don't you?"

"I can't help the way Casey wrote the story. I told him—"

The Navajo chimes over the door announced visitors. Blair focused toward them and smiled, so as not to appear rude to his mother's customers, but inside his head violent arguments raged. Hardly realizing he'd done it, he picked up the bottle of Orange Crush and drank it down in three long gulps.

Eventually the customers left, having debated for almost half an hour over a three-hundred-dollar sand painting and having bought, instead, four postcards and a two-dollar key chain with tiny moccasins attached. By the time they were gone Blair's mood had lifted of its own accord. He thought about riding a little while before supper but it seemed too much effort. He snapped open the cover on his braille watch and touched the face. Ten to five. Time for "Star Trek" reruns. He could flop on his bed and listen to that till supper. That sounded good.

"Let's close up," Norma said. She gathered her cash box and reading material while Blair put away their pop bottles, and together they emerged into the still-bright sunlight.

Sundance was coming. Blair heard the crunch of gravel in the rhythm of his horse's singlefoot gait. Suddenly he felt crabby again, felt the need to fight with someone, or to win a round against Loren somehow, just once. He dropped his arm around his mother's shoulders as they walked toward the sound of the approaching horse.

But as they stopped beside Sundance he felt her lean

away from him, to touch Loren. Stiffly he dropped his arm and stood away from her. She didn't notice.

"Where are you off to?" Norma asked.

"Just around." Loren's voice was cool, light. Infuriating.

"Not on my horse, you're not," Blair said suddenly.

"Why? You're not riding him. I already gave Kade his workout. I'm just going down the road a ways."

"Then go down the road on your own horse. You wanted the hotshot Arab and you got him, so leave the Kid to me." To cover the petulance of his words Blair hurried on. "You can ride the Kid back to the barn and I'll meet you there, and go down the road with you, okay? How long till supper, Mom?"

"It's just cold stuff tonight, hon. You boys ride as long as you want. If Dad and I get hungry we'll start without you." She raised her voice toward the departing Loren. "Just be back before dark. I don't want you riding those horses along the highway after dark, hear?"

As they started up the hill toward the house, Norma slipped her arm around Blair's waist. She said, hesitantly, "Blair, what you said about Kadir, does it bother you that Loren has him and you have Sundance Kid? I mean, I personally think Sundance is a ten times better horse than Kade, but, you know . . ."

"No. It doesn't really bother me." He wanted to say more, now, while she was listening and trying to understand, but his emotions were too tangled for quick sorting. He didn't want Kadir, he never rode him, he liked and trusted Sundance. So there was no reason for the anger he felt toward his brother and the flashy little Arab, no logical reason that could be explained even to himself, much less to a mother.

15

Ten minutes later Blair was in the saddle, and smiling. He rode erect and finely balanced, one hand holding the braided rawhide hackamore reins high and loose while the Kid swung his broad body into an ambling singlefoot gait. Ahead of them, Blair heard Kade's trotting rhythm periodically broken as the horse shied playfully. In the gentle swing of the body beneath him Blair found a gradual loosening of the tensions accumulated through the day.

Aahh . . . nice.

Suddenly the horses stopped, and girls' voices jarred Blair from his drifting pleasure.

"What are you guys doing out here?"

"Just riding," Loren said.

"Are those your horses? They're pretty. What are their names?" Two feminine voices. Blair struggled to recognize them, but couldn't.

Loren's voice bubbled and broke. "This one is El Kadir. He's an Arabian—"

"Half," Blair said.

"And that's my brother's horse, The Sundance Kid. He's just an old mustang but he's pretty nice. You girls want a ride?"

Silence.

Loren said, "Come on, we'll give you a ride up to the Taco Tree and back. You can leave your bikes in the ditch there, nobody'll bother them. Connie, you ride up here behind me, okay? Your hair'll just match the color of the horse."

Mumbling, giggling, then the clanging of dropped bicycles, and Blair felt a hand reaching up toward his saddle horn. Quickly he vacated his stirrup and hauled up whoever it was, until she was settled behind him, her hands on his hips.

"It's Erin Kepner," the girl said shyly. "You probably don't know me. I'm a sophomore."

"Well. I know you now. I'm Blair Liskey." His voice was rich with smiling. He assumed, since Loren had snatched up the other girl, that Erin was probably not the better catch of the two, but for the moment he didn't care. Those little hands felt good there on his belt. He leaned back slightly, into the circle of her arms, and discovered her breasts against his back.

"I read that story about you in the *Register*," Erin said. "Are you really going to ride a hundred miles?"

Blair leaned back some more, and began telling her about the Trek.

As they neared the bicycles on the return ride, Blair turned his head and whispered, "Would you go out with me sometime? We'd have to double with my brother so he could drive, but maybe Loren and your friend . . . ?"

"Yes. I'd like to." Her voice was soft and light.

Blair rode home singing.

Chapter 2

Loren Liskey was small and slight in comparison with his brother. Even the sixteen months' difference in their ages wasn't sufficient excuse for his size, in his opinion. His hair was dark like Blair's, but soft and straight and inclined to get in his eyes when he was hatless, which was as seldom as possible. His eyes were gray-green, a plus factor in a school where more than half of the students were of Spanish American or Indian descent and brown eyes were boringly common. He wasn't impressed with the rest of himself so far, but he did like his eyes and his clothes.

His hat was the classiest in Sears' western wear catalog, a brown felt hat with high crown, rolled brim, and pheasant feather band. The shirt was old and ordinary but the faded earth tones of its plaid made him feel cowboyish and hard-muscled. So did the supple tightness of his Levis and the feel of the ornate Justin Bulldoggers on his feet. Lately he'd begun having flashes of a sensation of living within a soft drink commercial, the dusty sunshine, the horses, mountains in the background, handsome young Westerner relishing the good life.

On the drive home from school he was aware that Blair was mad at him for forgetting to meet him at the lockers. He hadn't forgotten. He'd flat out wanted Blair to have to come looking for him. After the way that jerk hogged the glory about the Trek in the newspaper, Loren had told himself, let him find his own way to the truck. A little shot of humblehood was just what Blair needed.

He was glad to drop Blair at the shop, glad to escape the stifling emotions generated by too much closeness with Blair, especially right after Loren had shafted him. He spun the truck away from the shop with a satisfying clatter of gravel, but subdued the urge to peel rubber up the S-curved driveway that connected the shop to the house. He never knew what windows his mother might be watching from, still passing judgment on his maturity and responsibility behind the wheel.

The house sat on the crest of a mild slope above and behind the Navajo Shop. The original structure, now just the kitchen part, was adobe like the shop, with heavy lintel beams and thick walls that conquered sandstorms and summer heat. To the north and east jutted wings built of peeled, varnished logs and behind the house stretched a newer plank wing comprising a breezeway and double garage. In spite of its mismatched parts the little house managed to radiate comfort and welcome, and a sense of belonging where it sat. Cottonwoods leaned protectively over it and the double row of windbreak pines, planted three years ago in Neal Liskey's battle against wind and sand, were big enough now to give the feeling of shelter, even if they still failed in their duty in windstorm weather.

Loren parked the pickup outside, since its half of the garage was filled with lawn equipment and saddle racks,

and clumped into the house to deposit his books on the kitchen counter.

"I'm home," he yelled.

Pancho fluttered in his cage and sent a spray of gravel onto the kitchen floor, but there was no other answer. Loren got a can of Dr. Pepper from the refrigerator, opened it, and took a long luxurious pull. Pancho squawked, trilled, ended in something that might have been "Pretty bird."

"No you're not, you're a dirty mess." Loren passed the parakeet a gift, the tab from his pop can. Pancho snatched it, flew to his highest perch, and expertly tossed the bit of gleaming metal to the floor of his cage. He pounced, killed it, flew with it to the top perch, and repeated the game.

Loren watched for a while, then sighed, conscious of the horses waiting outside. He glanced down at himself. The shirt had been to school two days, and the jeans all week. Friday afternoon, no point in changing. He tossed back another long swig of Dr. Pepper and went out through the breezeway, can in hand, his legs bowing slightly as he got into his role. He went into the garage and emerged with his saddle slung over his shoulder, a battered split-ear bridle around his neck.

Across the backyard and just beyond the line of baby windbreaks was a rectangle of pasture, roughly twelve acres that ran along the highway in a block of unshaded green. The corner nearest to the house was fenced off in a small pole corral, and within the corral stood a three-sided shed, its open side away from the prevailing winds.

The horses stood inside the shed, seeking protection not from wind but from the sun. Loren heaved his saddle

20

onto the fence and stood looking at the four of them, wishing it were a half hour from now.

Four heads turned toward him with curiosity, affection, greed, or wary suspicion, depending on personalities and expectations. The suspicion was from Kade, who knew the saddle was meant for him. Suspicion showed also in Raven's eyes. He was seldom ridden, but lived in suspicion anyway. Sundance showed affection mixed inseparably with greed, and Daisy Mae was mildly curious at the interruption of her daydreaming, but only for a moment.

Loren and Kade eyed each other. Together they glanced at the corral gate, open to the pasture. Together they bolted toward it. Loren won by a hair, and the gate swung shut as Kade plowed to a stop, just bumping it with his nose.

"It's your own fault," Loren said crossly. "Why don't you just relax and be philosophical about it, like Dance?" He slipped inside the corral, snagged the lead rope from its nail in the shed, and tied Kade to the fence for a once-over with the brush and currycomb.

El Kadir was a liver chestnut, a dark red-brown all over, including his mane and tail. The richness of his color was intensified by a neat blaze on his face, and four high, white stockings. He was fifteen hands tall, slim and elegant of build, and arrogant in his treatment of the other horses. He seemed to know that he was the only one among them with any pretentions to braggable breeding, even though his background was considerably short of top class.

He had begun life on a small ranch near Wagon Mound, where horses were mass-produced for a market hungry for Arab, or part-Arab horses. The ranch's herd sire was a

21

purebred Arabian, purebred but little more than that in quality. The mares, and they were many, were mostly mustangs, cheap range mares, big-footed and coarse through the head and neck.

El Kadir had inherited a surprisingly Arabian appearance, all things considered, but what was inside the pretty, white-striped head was a less fortunate combination of genetics. Mustang craft and tough-headedness were blended with Arabian alertness and spirit, but without the leavening of sweetness and eagerness to please that should have gone with them.

In the hands of a tough, sure rider who enjoyed a tussle, El Kadir might have been an outstanding gaming or stock horse. But Loren Liskey was no match for him, and they both knew it.

Kade stood politely through the grooming, the saddling. He always did. Loren led him through the gate, and as the offside stirrup knocked against the gate post Kadir gathered himself and leaped, sweating and snorting in overdramatized fear.

"Gonna be one of those days, huh?" Loren soothed him, gathered his reins, and mounted. They started across the pasture in a sideways trot, extremely collected, a fun prancing gait except that Loren was uneasy about the way Kade was snatching at the bit.

"Why can't you just walk, like other horses?"

A car went by, and Loren was fleetingly aware of the picture he and Kade were making, elegant chestnut Arabian and slim, tough, handsome young man easily controlling him. He glanced toward the car. No one was watching.

His hands gave a fraction on the reins, and Kade surged

ahead in a fast straight trot. Much as he would have preferred the comfort of a canter, Loren didn't dare, yet. They trotted the length of the pasture, diagonally, then back again. Kade's neck was dark with sweat, but there was still too much spring in his movement. Around they went again, and again and again. Loren's legs ached with the effort of easing himself over the jarring trot.

Finally, when Kade seemed to be tiring, Loren pulled him down to a near walk, braced himself, and touched the horse into a canter.

Two canter strides, just enough to catch Loren off guard, then his head disappeared and he bucked.

"Damn you," Loren grunted as he hauled the head back up where it belonged, "you always do that to me. Well, you didn't get me off, this time. Now you settle down or you're going to the Alpo factory, you got that?"

They set off again at a collected canter, Kade's ears curving alertly up ahead. Just as Loren began to relax, Kade's head dipped. "Oh, no, you don't." Loren braced against the saddle horn and hauled up the head, so that the buck fizzled into a harmless, heads-up bounce.

They cantered on.

Suddenly Kade leaped sideways, and Loren hit the ground face first. A car went by, and slowed as the driver and passengers stared. Loren picked himself up, swatted off the dust on his shirt, and tried to ignore the audience beyond the fence. Kade stood waiting politely.

"You buzzard, you got me again, didn't you," Loren muttered as he stepped up into the saddle. The car drove on.

Having scored, Kade settled down and gave Loren a smooth, mannerly ride. Several times they circled and crisscrossed the pasture at a lope, a flat walk, a slow jog-trot. The sweat on Kadir's neck was from exertion now, rather than nerves. When Loren finally rode him into the corral and stripped off the saddle, it was with a sense of having equaled the score, if not of actually winning the contest.

While El Kadir lowered himself to the ground for a grunting, thrashing dust-roll, Loren turned with pleasure toward the buckskin gelding, who waited placidly within the shadow of the shed.

The Sundance Kid stepped forward, nodding, to accept his turn under the currycomb and brushes. He was a big horse, well over sixteen hands, with a broad head that seemed coarse compared to Kadir's, and feet of impressive proportion. His color was a pale buff, his mane, tail, lower legs, and dorsal stripe down his spine a muddy brown-black.

He had been bought originally for Loren, two years ago, then passed on to Blair when Kadir was purchased, because the whole family agreed that Sundance must be Blair's. Everyone agreed aloud, but Loren still raged silently, sometimes.

Sundance had served time for ten years as a dude ranch mount, carrying all kinds of riders with equal patience on pack trips and moonlight rides and elk hunts. He seldom made a hurried move, but never made a wrong one. Loren sometimes fancied that Sundance had always wanted a permanent family, a permanent master, and that now the placid beast lived his life in gratitude, aimed mostly at Loren, who took care of him.

"What do you say, buddy? Shall we ramble?" Loren snapped the lead rope onto the horse's halter, led him

24

through the gate, stepped up onto the fence, and from there leaped and sprawled across the yellow back. Out the pasture gate they went, Loren maneuvering the gate from above, and Sundance placing himself so that Loren could reach.

Loren smiled and settled in.

Ah.

Sundance picked up his favorite gait, an ambling single-foot that carried him faster than a walk, smoother than a trot, across the yard, through the concrete breezeway, and down the drive toward the shop.

Loren was just settling into the enjoyment of riding Sundance when he saw his mother and Blair emerging from the shop. She looked small and soft and somehow naive, in her too-loose jeans and too-dressy blouse, her beauty shop permanent that never seemed to have any special style to it. Blair's arm went around her shoulders and to Loren, looking down on them, they seemed disturbingly close. A closed corporation, Mom and Blair. His spirit darkened.

She grabbed the toe of his boot and shook his foot and made him feel better.

"Where are you off to?"

"Just around."

"Not on my horse you're not," Blair said, and with a long inward sigh Loren knew that Blair was going to claim Sundance. Loren's intention was to ride along the highway toward town. It was Friday afternoon, there'd be kids out goofing off, parking around the Taco Tree. On Sundance riding around up there would be fun, but not on Kadir. Not on a horse that spooked at birds, let alone Hondas and dual pipes.

25

But there was no way out. As always, Blair won the battle. He had weapons Loren couldn't begin to compete with.

Kade started off with uncharacteristic decorum, having been somewhat worn down by his pasture workout. And when Connie Cruz and her friend Erin Something appeared along the road Loren was suddenly glad he was astride the Arabian.

With Connie up behind him, Loren got gladder. Kade's little sideways leaps made Connie gasp and grab on hard around his waist, and gave Loren the chance to be masterful. He didn't get many chances.

"Would you let me ride him alone sometime?" Connie asked in his ear.

"Oh, I don't know. He's pretty much of a handful. Nobody rides him but me. But you could come out some time and use my brother's horse, and we could go for a nice long ride up in the mountains. Maybe take along a six-pack of beer and a blanket? That sound good?"

"Sounds pretty bad, Loren Liskey." She whapped him on the top of his hat.

He thought quickly. He'd never particularly noticed Connie before since she wasn't in any of his classes, but up close she was pretty cute, all that long dark curly hair and everything. Wouldn't do his reputation any harm to be seen with this one. And she was getting pretty cuddly back there, even though Kade was just walking quietly now.

"Okay then," he said, "how about if I came and got you in a couple hours and we drove around a while, hit the Taco Tree or whatever. Okay?"

She hesitated a moment. "How about if Blair and Erin come too?"

He shook his head. No way, he thought. I've been my brother's keeper as long as I can stand, this week. Tonight's for me. "Won't work. My dad won't be home with the car, and we couldn't get four in the pickup."

"Soup's on, come and get it or I'll throw it away." Norma's cheerful call brought the boys from their respective rooms and her husband from the "CBS Evening News" in the livingroom. On Blair's shoulder rode the green and yellow parakeet. Loren walked with his face in a book and groped his way into his chair without losing his place.

Neal Liskey was a small, neatly polished man who tried to compensate for his lack of stature with meticulous grooming, and nearly succeeded. His kinky dark hair never moved, his shirts never looked wrinkled, even though he seldom changed from business clothes to casual dress in the evenings.

He asked the blessing, then looked around the table. "Blair, ditch the bird," he said.

"He'll stay on my shoulder."

Loren looked up from his book. "No he won't. He always ends up on the table, and he leaves doo-doos."

Norma said "Lorey."

Sighing heavily, Blair got up and shrugged Pancho off into his cage. Loren watched, smiling, until he met his father's eyes.

"And you, young man, you know the rule about reading at the table."

"I wasn't really reading it," Loren said quickly. "This is the book on distance riding that I ordered. It just came today. It's really neat, Dad, it tells how to take a horse's pulse and respiration and everything. That's what we'll have to do when we start conditioning our horses for the Trek. The only thing is, my watch doesn't have a second hand on it, and I'm going to need one, to take the readings with. Do you think I could get a new watch, just a cheap one? Or a stopwatch?"

Neal dollopped a mound of potato salad onto his plate and passed the bowl to Blair. "No, not unless you intend to pay for it yourself. But I'll tell you what, I'll trade watches with you for the summer, how'd that be?"

Loren grinned. "Great. Thanks."

Norma said suddenly, "I know what let's. Let's all saddle up and go for a ride after supper, like we used to. We haven't done that for a long time, and we'll have an hour or so before dark. We can leave the dishes for later. Want to?"

Loren said, "Can't. I've got a date after while."

"Oh?" Norma said brightly. "Who with? Jennifer again?"

"No, Connie Cruz. She's a sophomore. We were giving her and her girl friend rides on the horses this aft."

Blair's head snapped up. He started to push his chair back. "Let me go call Erin and we'll go with you guys, okay?"

"Can't." Loren shook his head and thought frantically. "Erin's going with a guy from Wagon Mound. I asked Connie, I thought we could double, too, but she said Erin's really hooked on this guy."

The eagerness drained from Blair's face. "That's funny. I sort of asked her if she'd go out with me sometime and she more or less said yes. I mean, she sounded like she wanted to."

Loren looked down at his plate and wished he didn't have to do this in front of a parental audience. "Well, you know, buddy . . ."

"No. I don't know. What?"

"She probably felt sorry for you, you know, didn't want to hurt your feelings . . ."

"She could have just told me she was going with someone." Blair's voice was tight with rage.

"Now, boys," Norma said. "Blair, you come riding with Dad and me after supper, want to? We haven't done that for a long time. Okay? Want to?"

Blair shook his head and left the table.

Neal said, "If you want the car tonight, let me get some stuff out of the back before you take off."

"Okay," Loren said absently. Then, "No, er, that's okay, Dad, I'll take the truck. We're just going to hang around the Tree for a while. No big deal."

Loren's watch said twenty till midnight. The Cruzes' porch light reflected gold ribbons on the truck's hood. Beside the driveway, an old lilac hedge dipped its fragrant clusters near Loren's elbow. In the curve of his right arm Connie sighed and snuggled closer.

A good Friday night, Loren reflected. Lots of action around the Tree, lots of guys without dates cruising, calling, waving, watching him with Connie, shouting smart-mouth remarks that Connie fielded in good spirit. It was fun. She liked him. She let him go far enough to be exciting but not so far as to be scary. It was just the kind of Friday night he liked.

29

But Blair was there. Over all the best moments of the evening Blair's face superimposed itself, Blair's face with the eagerness draining out of it, the quickly hidden disappointment and bitterness. Whatever Loren had enjoyed of the evening, he knew his brother would have enjoyed doubly because the pleasure would have been rarer, for Blair. He so seldom allowed himself to show his interest in a datable girl, Loren reflected. He's had that mother-fixation, or whatever it is, on Mrs. Blanco all these years, and he talks a good game about girls in general, but an actual date? Almost never, so far. And he would have, tonight, if I wasn't such a horse's ass. Why do I *do* things like that to him. God. He's my brother! I'm supposed to love him, and I go and do things like this. Liskey, you're such a screw-up.

Chapter 3

"Nobody wants to go for a ride, huh?" Norma said wistfully as the family wandered away from the supper table. "Okay, then, I guess I'll . . . do the dishes." But no one was listening.

Blair went into his room and shut the door. His mood had been darkening steadily all through supper, and he was sick and tired of being down. He threw himself onto the bed, shoulders propped against the headboard, and laced his fingers across his stomach.

Okay, Liskey, let's think this through till we come out the other side. Is it Erin? Yeah, kind of. Why, because she made out like she wanted to go out with you? Maybe she did. Maybe she broke up with the guy in Wagon Mound, or maybe he never even existed. Maybe Connie just said that because she didn't want to double-date. Or maybe Loren said it so he wouldn't have to drag you along on his date. It would be easy enough to find out. All you have to do is call Erin and ask her.

He grinned suddenly.

Can't. Can't remember what her last name was. Okay

then, forget about it. What else is bugging you? What Loren said about Erin feeling sorry for you?

No. Yes. Well a little, maybe. That, and Mrs. Blanco . . .

Gradually he dug through to the bottom layer of the bad mood and faced it.

The college thing.

For almost an hour Blair lay staring into his thoughts. Finally, cramped by his hunch-shouldered position and the endless round of answerless questions in his head, he stretched and padded into the livingroom on the thick soles of his boot socks.

His parents were curled on the davenport together watching the opening credits of the eight o'clock movie. Blair felt their closeness and wanted, suddenly, to burrow his six-foot frame in between them, as he'd done when he was little.

"Dad, are you watching the movie? Could I talk to you about something?"

The remote control clicked the sound of the movie down. Not off, just down.

"It's important, Dad, both of you."

The set clicked off then, and Blair heard the two of them sitting up, rearranging themselves to listen to him. He sat cross-legged on the floor.

"I've been thinking about my future."

Norma leaned forward. "What brought that on, honey?"

"I don't know. Something Mrs. Blanco said today. Well, one thing she said was that I wouldn't be needing her after this year."

"That's good news," Neal said, and Norma squeezed Blair's knee. "You'll miss her, won't you? She's been a good friend to you ever since fifth grade."

"Yeah. Well, she said something today about me going to college, you know, needling me like she does. She kind of made a crack about me selling pencils on a street corner and I made a crack back about selling Navajo craft on a highway corner. Mom, does that shop make much money? I mean, is it anything a person could make a real living at? I know it's always been your baby, but I was thinking, maybe if we built onto it or added some other kind of thing, like a snack shop or gas station . . . I wouldn't have any trouble running the Navajo Shop . . ."

His voice trailed away. He could read in his mother's silence her dislike of the idea of sharing her shop. It *was* her baby, her hobby, her financial security and independence and Christmas present money.

Quickly Blair said, "Or another thing I was thinking about. Dad, remember when we first bought this place and moved here, you kept talking about what a good spot it would be for a motel. Remember? No competition any closer than Wagon Mound, and it could be a really good family business. You could even quit Xerox if you wanted to, or kind of retire to the motel business, and I could run the front desk. There wouldn't be anything to that that I couldn't manage, or figure out ways of doing. If we started working on the plans now, we could have it all built and ready to go by the time I'm out of school."

Blair listened to the silence and tried to read it.

Neal cleared his throat. "Couple of things wrong with that plan, Blair. For one thing, do you have any idea how much it would cost, at today's prices, to build and equip a motel?"

"Well geeze, Dad, it doesn't have to be the Rebano Hilton. I just meant a nice little . . ."

"Even a nice little. We just don't have that kind of money lying around."

"No, not lying around, I mean I know that. But you could swing a bank loan. You make good money. And I thought that was kind of what you guys had in mind when you bought this place. Fifteen acres along the highway . . ."

Norma said softly, "We did talk about it for a while there, but it would just cost so much. We'd be in debt the rest of our lives. And there's not really enough tourist traffic up this little old road. We found that out with the Navajo Shop. We thought that was going to be a gold mine, and maybe even make enough to help finance the building of a little motel. But it just hasn't worked out that way. It averages maybe forty, fifty dollars a week, profits. Just about enough to keep you guys and me in pocket money."

Blair was surprised into silence. Forty bucks a week, with all the time she put in down there?

Neal said, "Years ago I did think I'd like to be my own boss but, I don't know, I've been with the company almost twenty years now, they've got a good retirement program and Blue Cross and all, and it's a safe, steady income. And besides, I like what I'm doing, and I'm good at it. I can troubleshoot any office copier that company puts out, and I can do it better than anybody else in Northeast New Mexico. I wouldn't want to give that up."

"Even for me?" Blair asked in a voice much too small for his size. "Even to help me get started in a business I could run for the rest of my life, and raise a family of my own on?"

Neal's voice came out hard and even. "If we honestly thought it would be best for you, your mother and I would

34

hock our souls to build you a motel to run. But it wouldn't be good for you, don't you see that? It would be too easy, just staying home, coasting along on something you could learn to do in a week, when what you really need is to get out on your own, go to college, use that good brain of yours to learn a real profession. You can do anything you want, Blair, if you'll just push yourself forward a little, and try."

He stood up. "I don't guess I need to push myself, everybody else is doing it for me. Thank you one and all for your fine support."

"Blair, you don't . . ." Norma's reprimand was cut short by the telephone. Blair, being closest, answered it.

"Hello . . . yes, this is him. Who? Really? Um, yeah, I guess it would be okay. Sure, I'd be glad to. Yeah, okay. Bye."

He turned to his parents, grinning. "That was some lady from the Albuquerque Sunday paper. She read the story about me in the Rebano paper and she wants to do a picture story about me doing the Trek. Isn't that great? Ole Loren's going to be so jealous he'll choke."

It wasn't until much later, when Loren was home from his date and the house was finally still, that Blair, lying restlessly in a tangle of sheets, realized fully what he had done. He was committed now, beyond all hope of backing out, to going through with the Trek.

For a long time he lay there projecting mental images and testing himself against them. Riding in a place where the terrain was completely unknown, riding not in the home pasture or along the road with Loren or Mom or Dad just a horse-length ahead but in some lofty mountain range with narrow trails, fatally steep drop-offs . . . the possibility of getting separated from Loren. Above all, the terrifying possibility of being left alone.

Can I do it? God I don't *know.*

Blair walked into the kitchen the next morning, and into the charged current of Loren's impatience.

"It's nine o'clock. I was about ready to come in after you. We've got a lot to do this morning, hermano, we've got to get cracking, man."

Blair rubbed his knuckles across his scalp in an attempt to waken his sleep-fuzzed brain. Yawning, he opened the refrigerator and located the orange juice bottle. "What do we have to do this morning, according to you?"

Loren ignored the sarcasm. "I've been studying this book on distance riding, the part about conditioning your horse. It says the first thing you should do is rate your horse over a marked distance at his average walk, trot, and canter, so you can compute your times and distances in your head during the ride. Also, we'll have to be able to guess how far we go on our training rides, so we'll need to know our horses' speeds at their various gaits. I thought we could do that this morning, okay?"

Blair shrugged. He fixed himself a dish of Shredded Wheat and sat down. "Okay. You're the chief. How do we do it?"

"We're all set up for it already. While you were in there sleeping I took the truck up to Kenn's road and measured off a half mile, and laid two sets of tire chains across the road to mark it. I figured you could hear if Sundance stepped on the chains, or feel it in his stride if he hops over them. Hurry up and eat, will you?"

An uneasiness began in Blair's stomach. "You mean we

36

each have to measure our horses separately? Why can't we just ride together?"

"No," Loren said firmly. "If we're going to do this job right, we have to know the speeds of both of our horses' gaits separately. You can do it, it's just a straight road."

As Blair rose to put his dishes in the sink he felt doubly angry, at himself for the twist of fear in his stomach at the prospect of riding alone, and at Loren for perceiving that fear. While he saddled Sundance and followed Loren and Kade out of the yard and down the road, Blair repeated to himself over and over, It's a straight, flat, dead-end road with no traffic. Sundance can see where he's going. There's nothing to worry about.

Past the Navajo Shop and a quarter mile down the road, a dirt track led to the left, toward a now-empty ranch house a mile from the highway. The boys had ridden down it often.

"You wait here," Loren said. "I'll walk him to the chains and back, and see how long it takes. Then you can do Sundance."

"Why don't we do them both together?" Blair asked.

"Because that wouldn't give us an honest reading." Loren sounded impatient. "I already explained. If we timed them together, the slow horse would hold the fast one back, and I want to know their individual times."

"But on the Trek we'll be together all the time, so what difference does it make? And on the training rides."

"We might get separated, who knows? Anyway, I want to do this right. Okay now, ready . . . set . . . here I go."

Sundance tried to follow Kade. When Blair held him back, he dropped his head and began grazing at the road-side.

37

We might get separated. Blair remembered the time, five or six years ago, when he had found himself seated beside Loren in a roller coaster car, at Elitch's Gardens in Denver, during a vacation trip. Loren had begged to go on the ride, and Blair, being a year and a half older, hadn't dared to say he didn't want to. As the car had begun to move, to rattle and clang and pick up speed for the first terrible climb, Blair was overwhelmed by a sense of on-rushing terror and helplessness. He was in the train. He was powerless to stop it.

A shadow of that feeling came over him as he heard Kade's hoofbeats approaching.

"Hey, wow, he did it in a little under ten minutes," Loren chirped. "That means he walks, let's see . . ."

"Six miles an hour," Blair said. "That's pretty fast, isn't it?"

"It sure is. The book says most horses walk at an average of three to five miles an hour. So six is really fast. Well, he kept trying to run. I had to keep pulling him back down to a walk, so he probably gained a fraction on me, there. Still, that's awful good time. Okay now, your turn. Get him out here. There now, you're headed pretty straight, no, more to the right. There. Okay, ready . . . set . . . go."

Sundance moved out reluctantly. Several times he tried to turn back toward Kade. Being Blair's horse, he was an habitual follower and in his placid way he objected to going out on his own. For the first few minutes Blair was kept busy straightening Sundance's course along the road in response to Loren's shouts of "Left, left, no, right now. Now you're straight."

But when Sundance descended the first shallow dip in the road and lost sight of Kade in his peripheral vision he ceased his attempts to return and settled into a plodding walk. Some of the tension drained out of Blair then.

This isn't too bad. I can do this.

He settled into the rocking rhythm of the saddle and began to enjoy the solitude, the sense of delicious aloneness that came to him so seldom, surrounded as he usually was with helpers. A hawk called, high and to the right, and in the distance lambs bleated.

But the minutes ticked away, the plodding walk went on, and Sundance's hooves struck no tire chains. Blair touched the face of his watch and frowned. Eight minutes. Already they'd spent almost as much time as Kade used for the whole mile, and they weren't even to the halfway point.

Unless we went past it. Unless he stepped over the chains and I didn't know it, or we're off to the side of the road and he went around the chains. Should we turn around? Keep going a little farther?

Just as he grew certain that he had missed the chains and was far past them Blair heard and felt the contact of metal shoe against chain. He got off and felt on the ground to be sure it really was a tire chain. It was. He checked his watch again. Ten minutes. As he remounted and started back he computed the figures.

There was no getting around it. Sundance had a three-mile-an-hour walk. Half the speed of Kade. A small new fear lodged itself deep in Blair's mind, but he refused to look at it.

Going back, he cheated a little and allowed the now-eager Sundance to slip up into his singlefoot gait part of the way, so Loren wouldn't know how much slower Dance really was.

The trotting times for the two horses showed an equal disparity. El Kadir's reaching stride brought him around the mile in six minutes, giving him an excellent trot speed of ten miles an hour. Sundance jogged home in nearly double the time. He didn't like to trot; he preferred to singlefoot or lope, and Blair rode the trot sloppily so that his weight bounced down on Dance's kidneys with every step.

Blair's riding was sloppy because he was insecure. His leg muscles weren't accustomed to the strain of standing in the stirrups to ease the jolt of the trot and his balance was suddenly nonexistent. The increased speed made him tense and hunch into an off-center position, and dips in the road, unnoticeable at the slower walk, now seemed to tip the horse under him just as the roller coaster cars had tilted without warning.

"Okay, now cantering," Loren said brightly. "And remember, we should hold it to a slow lope rather than a gallop. Just a nice safe trail-speed lope, okay? Here I go."

Blair listened to the retreating three-beat rhythm of Kade's canter. Just before it faded from earshot it was interrupted by a sliding sound and the thud of Loren hitting the ground. Blair hesitated, listened, started to rein Sundance toward the sound. But the sound of Loren's swearing stopped him, and in another second the canter beat resumed.

"At least I don't have to worry about that kind of nonsense with you, do I?" He ran his hand down Sundance's mane. "You might not burn a hole in the wind with your speed, old buddy, but at least you're not going to be trying to dump me."

Blair's canter turn proved to be less frightening than

40

he'd expected. By now Sundance knew the routine and slipped willingly into his rocking chair lope, turned back without cueing at the chains, and loped home again in a passable thirteen miles an hour. Blair rode tensely at first, but soon found himself relaxing, trusting Sundance. He was prepared for the dips in the road this time and even felt a mild exhilaration when Sundance rocked up a shallow slope and Blair's body automatically canted into balance position.

The boys jogged home, tire chains jangling from Sundance's saddle horn. Blair felt relief, even pride, at having survived the solo riding, but he was also aware of aching legs and back. And that was just three miles, he thought grimly. How am I ever going to do fifty in a day, two days in a row?

He heard Loren flip open the pocket notebook in which he'd recorded their speeds. "Boy," Loren muttered, "I never realized before how fast Kade is. And how slow the Kid is. You're really going to hold me back on the Trek."

"Maybe not," Blair bristled. "Once upon a time there was this tortoise and this hare, and while the hare was wasting his energy spooking all over the trail and bucking his rider off every time they tried to canter, that old tortoise just kept on keeping on, and you know who won that race, don't you?"

Loren snorted. "That's not the point," he said as he always did when Blair was too near the point. "The point is, you don't have a chance of winning the junior division trophy no matter how fast your tortoise goes, because you've always got to be behind me. And you don't care about winning it anyway, just about completing the ride. But for me it's different, see? Kade made really good times

41

this morning. I think he and I would have a good shot at winning junior division if we didn't have to hang back so you could keep up. I know what. Maybe we can find some other slow horse in junior division that you could ride along with."

Blair said nothing, but his pleasure at overcoming the morning's obstacles faded. Loren didn't want him on the Trek. He could hear the plotting in his brother's smooth, bright tones. An odd sort of apprehension settled over him, as if he were being drawn into a war-game in which he knew neither the rules nor the object.

When lunch was over and Loren had disappeared, Blair said, "Mom, if I come down to the shop with you this afternoon, would you read me Loren's distance riding book?"

"If you want me to," she said slowly, "but why bother? As long as Loren knows what to do, isn't that enough?"

No. But he couldn't tell her why, nor did he understand, himself, why he suddenly felt that he needed to arm himself with information independent of what Loren told him.

He and Norma settled into their chairs in the shop, and she opened the book.

" 'Introduction. What is distance riding? It is a sport as old as our country, as old as man's partnership with the horse. In recent years it has grown into one of the most exciting and popular forms of fun on horseback.

" 'First we must differentiate between endurance and competitive trail riding, as this point causes much confusion to newcomers. Endurance riding is a race. The first rider in is the winner, provided his mount passes the final physical check. Competitive rides are won by the horse who finishes within a specified time limit, in the best physical condition and with the best all-round score, judged on such things as way of going, trail manners, etc. In addition to this basic difference, endurance rides are held over a longer distance, usually fifty to a hundred miles but sometimes as much as three hundred miles, while competitive rides usually average twenty-five to forty miles.' "

Norma looked up. "The Sangre Trek would be an endurance ride then, right?"

"Right. Skip over the parts about competitive. Just give me the endurance stuff."

As she read, Blair listened intently and stored the new knowledge as though it were artillery.

Chapter 4

During the following week Loren tried to put the Trek aside and concentrate on final tests, on getting out of eleventh grade with a higher grade average than Blair's. It was a losing battle, he knew. No matter how much better Loren's final grades might be, he could never really compete with a blind brother. Blair simply got so much more *credit* for every little thing he did. Like the book reports in English. Blair got to do his verbally instead of having to hand in a neatly typewritten five pages. No points off for spelling or punctuation or paragraphing. All he had to do was stand up there and smile and rattle off a little bit of resumé and analysis, and he got an A. Loren knew, without a doubt, that his own B-plus report had been better. It was better thought out, better constructed, and had cost him much more work time.

But you didn't have to read your book one slow word at a time on a machine, a nasty voice reminded him, and he flared back, But that shouldn't *count*.

It did, though. And everything seemed to count in Blair's favor.

Through the week, in the spaces of thinking time that weren't swallowed up by school work, Loren was aware of an unpleasant feeling that had started sometime Saturday morning while he and Blair had been rating the horses. It was a growing awareness of Kade's potential to place well, possibly even to win the junior division of the Trek . . . if it weren't for Sundance holding him back. In the dark core of this unpleasant feeling was the knowledge that Loren did not want Blair on that endurance ride.

But the ride was Blair's idea in the first place. He was the one who had heard about it from a guy at school whose cousin had come down from Colorado to compete in the Trek last year. It was Blair who had first talked about the two of them doing the ride, and it was Blair who had contacted the guy's cousin for the address of the organization holding the ride.

Loren had only been included in order to make it possible for Blair to showcase his blindness. And it was working out just as Blair wanted it to, Loren thought bitterly. First the story in the local paper, then the reporter from the Albuquerque paper wanting to do the story on him. And, as always, good ole baby brother was way in the background.

Loren could pinpoint in his memory the exact moment he had known that he could never compete with Blair and win. It was nine years ago, on Mother's Day. With pride and anticipation glowing on his small face, Loren had offered up his love-sacrifice. It was an ashtray. The second graders had been given a choice of presents to make for their mothers, ashtrays made of coiled snakes of clay, prints of their hands in clay, or silhouettes of themselves

45

cut out of black paper and pasted onto white. Loren had chosen the ashtray because it entailed by far the most work.

First he'd had to roll the clay back and forth between his hands to make it into a long snake of even thickness. But it kept getting thin toward the bottom, then the rolling motion made the end whip around and break off at the thin place. Time and again he'd had to patch it back together before the snake was long enough. Then, with Mrs. Miller directing over his shoulder, he'd started a tight coil, pressing the clay against itself until he'd gone around four times, making the bottom of the ashtray. Then, ever so carefully, his tongue held hard between his teeth, Loren had started the fifth round atop the fourth, pinching it into place with his fingers, building up and up around the edges until the snake of clay was actually a bowl, with bottom and sides.

He'd stroked and stroked with his fingers until the coils disappeared and became smooth, flat sides. He pinched a lip on either side for the cigarettes to lie in and, painstakingly, he wrote on the bottom with a toothpick, "Happy Mother's Day From Loren. I Love You." It was definitely one of the best ashtrays to go into the kiln, and after it had been dipped in white paint with green paint dribbled around the rim to make a pattern, it was perfect.

Mother's reaction that Sunday morning was all Loren hoped for . . . until she opened her second package. In it was a crude clay plaque with Blair's handprint in it and "Blair 1973" scratched around the bottom. Loren watched and listened with growing dismay as his mother praised the ugly thing. Even though Blair went to the School for the Blind and was a year ahead of Loren, Loren knew what went into the making of that plaque. It had to be the same, no matter what school or grade you were in. You made a ball of clay and rolled it out and smashed your hand in the middle and wrote your name around the edge. It was easy. His classmates who had made hands were finished with their projects and doing workbooks while Loren and the other ashtray-makers were still making their snakes.

Loren stood beside the diningroom table and stared with big solemn eyes as his mother wrapped her arms around Blair and held him close and ran her fingertips over the plaque.

Later, when she was in the kitchen, Loren found Blair standing with the ashtray in his hands, feeling it.

"You're dumb," Blair said. "She doesn't like ashtrays."

Loren stopped as though he'd been punched. It was true. It was *true*. Neither she nor Daddy smoked cigarettes, and Loren remembered her telling someone that she didn't keep ashtrays around the house because it only encouraged visitors to light up and make her house smell bad.

Without thought Loren launched himself at his big brother, fists flailing. Blair howled and began hitting back and the ashtray fell to the rug and rolled to safety under the table.

"Loren, stop it! What's gotten into you?" Both parents pulled the boys apart, both parents scolded, but it was the horror in his mother's voice that stabbed Loren. It didn't matter that Blair had started it or that Loren had been goaded beyond endurance by Blair's knowledge of his stupidity. What did matter was that Loren Liskey was the kind of little boy who would hit his blind brother.

Unforgivable.

47

The Blair handprint was hung on the kitchen wall. The Loren ashtray was retrieved and used as a nut dish, and eventually the incident was forgotten by everyone but Loren. In the intervening years there had been other competitions, secret competitions that no one but Loren knew about or understood: the fierceness of the smaller boy at arm wrestling or Monopoly, the vying for parental attention, and later, when Blair joined Loren in his class at public school, the continued attempts to outshine Blair in the eyes of his teachers.

But it was impossible. Blair was forever conspicuous, needing the teacher's aide to read to him, getting excused from dull work to go have his session with Mrs. Blanco, being so damned *sweet* and *helpless* and *brave*. There was no way, ever, to strike at a brother like that without being a terrible person yourself. The frustration was overwhelming sometimes.

With maturity Loren's need to prove himself against Blair's measure remained as strong as ever, although it sought subtler forms than arm wrestling. He was haunted by the knowledge that Blair, blind, was a more valuable person than he was even with vision. Now, with the end of their high school years coming into view and bringing an enforced end to the competition, with each of them going off to pursue separate careers, Loren felt more tensely than ever that it must not end in a stalemate. He must, just once, outdo Blair at something, earn some praise for himself, some autonomy that had nothing to do with being Blair Liskey's brother.

The Trek. It would have to be the Trek. The junior division trophy would do it. But with Blair and Sundance dragging at him like an anchor, no way, José.

*   *   *

The four of them started out after breakfast on Friday,
Kade bearing Loren in the lead, with snorts at shadows,
Blair and The Sundance Kid placidly jogging behind. It
was the first day of vacation and of Loren's training program. In his shirt pocket he carried a tiny spiral notebook
and pen; on his wrist was Neal's watch; and in his head
were exciting figures and plans. They rode past the shop
and started down the road toward the old Kenn place,
where they had permission to use the pasture as their
training ground.

Loren pulled Kade back beside Sundance and said,
"Okay now, here's the game plan. We have eight weeks
till the ride and in that time we have to get the horses
muscled up, and their lungs and hearts strengthened, to
the point where they can do fifty miles in ten hours or
less without getting sored or lamed in any way. And they'll
have to be conditioned to the point where their pulses
and respiration will be near normal after a ten to fifteen
minute rest."

"I know all that," Blair said.

Loren's expression tightened. He knew Mom had been
reading his distance-riding book to Blair and he hated it.
He hated losing that advantage. But there was no way to
deny permission, no acceptable way, so he'd been forced
to content himself with knowing the book better than
Blair did, memorizing the figures and outlining the training program and going on with the presumption of leader-
ship.

He went on. "What we'll do is start out riding three
hours a day and work up gradually from there, increasing
our riding time as the horses get toughened up to it."

49

"And us, too," Blair grinned.

"Yeah, right. We'll have to do a lot of it at a trot, and that's going to take leg muscles on our part. I thought we'd start today with three hours of alternate walking and trotting, depending on the terrain, with a ten-minute rest stop after each hour, and we'll take their pulse and respiration readings before we go on. If the PRs are too high, we'll ease off a little. That sound okay with you?"

"You're the chief," Blair said cheerfully.

The empty Kenn house was small and cheaply built, and in the final stages of decay. The barn and sheds all leaned to the windward and the fences were held up only by the weeds. Loren dismounted and tied Kade's reins to the sagging pasture gate.

"One thing we'll have to start doing," he said, "is leaving the horses' halters on under their bridles and carrying tie ropes so when we stop we can take off their bridles and let them graze, and also so we won't run the risk of broken bridles from tying by the reins. I noticed all the horses in the pictures in the book were wearing halters and bridles both." A small satisfaction warmed Loren. At least the illustrations in the book were his.

"Now," he said somewhat officiously, "I'll check their PRs so we'll know what their normal readings are, and then we'll recheck after an hour of riding."

"I can do Dance's," Blair said. Was there a strand of steel in his voice?

Loren hesitated but could think of no good reason not to let Blair do his own readings. "Okay, then. We'll do pulse first. Feel up under Dancer's jawbone, right up here somewhere in that hollow. There's supposed to be an artery that you can feel a pulsebeat in. Got it?"

"No."

It took both boys a few minutes to locate the pulse point. Kade kept tossing his head, impatient at so much standing still. But finally they were ready.

"Okay now," Loren said, "I'll time us for fifteen seconds and you can count the beats of the pulse. Not out loud though, or you'll throw me off. Okay, here we go. Ready . . . set . . . count. . . . Stop. How many did you get?"

"Eight," Blair said. "Times four, is thirty-two beats a minute. That's about normal, according to the book. How about Kade?"

"About the same." But Loren frowned as he wrote Kade's actual pulse count in his notebook. Fifty-two. Quite a bit higher than the book said was normal for a horse at rest. He checked his arithmetic again. Thirteen beats times four quarter-minutes. Yep. Fifty-two all right. No need to tell Blair though, and give him the satisfaction.

Briskly he said, "Okay now, respiration. Cup your hand over Dance's nostril and count the puffs of his breath. Ready . . . go."

Sundance's respiration rate was eight; Kade's thirty-six. According to the book, normal range was from seven to twenty-five. A new fear assailed Loren. What if Kade turned out to be one of those horses the book warned about, an animal so excitable that his readings were dangerously high and didn't come back to normal levels in the time allotted? If Kade's PR readings didn't drop below seventy/forty after exertion, or if the figures went into inversion, with respiration higher than pulse, it would mean elimination from the race.

As they mounted and rode into the pasture Loren's thoughts followed this depressing channel. If Kade were

51

eliminated because of high readings, or for any other reason for that matter, it would be Loren's failure even though it wasn't his fault. And if that happened, there was always a possibility that some other rider would offer to help Blair through the rest of the race, and Blair would go on to victory in a blaze of glory, not the victory of winning the race but just of completing it, blind.

Loren's determination redoubled. He thought, Listen, horse, it's you and me, buddy. I'm going to make you the best-conditioned horse in that damn race and you're going to keep your readings down, and not buck me off some mountaintop, you got that?

The Kenn pasture sprawled for miles across rolling foothills between Rebano and the easternmost range of the Sangre de Christos. It was sandy grassland dotted with cottonwoods and crisscrossed by small streams and dry gulches that were former stream beds. On the higher slopes sheep and deer trails climbed among outcroppings of granite and there were some areas of rock slides and steep drops. But for the most part the land was benign. The ranch hadn't been worked since the Kenns died three years ago but another neighbor was leasing the grazing rights for a flock of Merinos.

Loren led the way at a brisk trot, a speed that he estimated to be Kade's ten-mile-an-hour gait. He scanned the landscape with a businesslike squint, choosing the best footing available. Within a very few minutes the muscles of his calves and thighs ached with the strain of bearing his weight up and out of the saddle. "Ride light and forward," the book had warned repeatedly. "Make your horse's work as easy as humanly possible. Remember, he has to do the actual work, so it's up to you to help him with every ounce of strength you have. Bounce on his back, ride over his kidneys, and he'll never make the distance."

On they trotted. Loren's leg muscles weakened from ache to unbearable. He glanced at his watch. Twenty minutes they'd been riding. Twenty lousy minutes. Forty more to go before they could stop and get off. He pulled Kade down to a walk for a few minutes, then they resumed the trot. Behind him, he heard the rhythm of Sundance's easy lope. He longed to put Kade into a canter, to relax into the easy rhythm of it and rest his legs, but he knew Kade's canter was not a time to relax. The instant he lowered his guard, Kade would lower his head, and Loren knew his legs were too weak to grip the saddle if Kade bucked now.

And besides—a grin suddenly crept across Loren's face— and besides, the book had warned against depending on the canter, or lope, as a trail gait for distance riding. Too much pressure on the leading front leg during that instant, on each stride, when the horse's entire weight was balanced on one front foot.

A horse could go lame on an overworked front leg if he cantered too much.

At the end of the hour Loren called a halt and they dismounted in the shade of a hillside cottonwood. His legs barely supported him as he stepped to Kade's head, but he noticed that Blair seemed to be moving normally. He hasn't been standing a trot for the last hour, Loren grumbled silently.

They checked the horses' readings; forty-eight/twenty for Sundance, eighty/eighty for Kade. High. Awfully high, Loren thought nervously. Almost inverted. Both horses were blowing and sweating, but Sundance dropped his head to the grass and began grazing almost immediately, while Kade simply stood.

The boys sat on the ground, holding their reins and following their horses' movements, Loren with wary eyes, Blair with his ears.

"How do you feel?" Loren asked suddenly.

"Fine as frog's hair. How about you?"

"My legs are killing me. All that standing to Kade's trot. That's going to make an old man out of me before next week. You're lucky you can just rock along in Dance's nice slow lope and not have to stand up."

He glanced sideways at Blair just in time to see his brother's expression grow wary. That was one thing about Blair, Loren thought. You could always read what he was thinking, all over his face. Damn.

Blair said, "But according to that book you're always quoting, cantering can break a horse down, if you do too much of it. I guess I'll have to follow your good example and start making him trot. Won't I?"

Loren shrugged and turned away. "Up to you. He's your horse. And you read the book."

The silence grew thick with things unsaid.

Over the next two weeks subtle changes began to show in Kade and Sundance. Upper leg muscles began to harden. Sundance's flanks lost their rounded contours and took on an angled appearance and he began holding his head a degree or two higher than before. Loren noticed that when Kade had a good trotting workout first, he bucked less frequently than before as he went into a canter.

Blair lost six pounds those first two weeks and his skin took on a rosy tan. Loren lost no weight but when he lay in bed at night rubbing his aching legs, there was a new hardness in his calves and thighs. He relished it. He felt as though his heart and lungs, along with Kade's, were growing larger, stronger, every day.

As June grew hotter, the three-hour riding sessions began earlier in the mornings. Blair and Loren began waking naturally between five and five-thirty, as the sky lightened, and were often in the saddle by six. Much of the time they rode wordlessly, conserving their energy for getting themselves and their horses through the three hours. As human and equine muscles began to toughen, the riding time seemed to shrink until the three-hour ride became an invigorating workout rather than a mountainous obstacle to be overcome. The trotting strides of both horses lengthened and smoothed as the days passed. Loren found himself often slipping into a state of near-trance engendered by the rhythm of the horse beneath him, rhythm that beat on steadily mile after mile, up hill, down hill, through the blazing New Mexico sun.

Kade's PR readings remained high, much higher than Sundance's, but they never went beyond the danger point and gradually Loren ceased to worry about them. Kade was simply a more excitable animal than Sundance, he told himself. That was all it was.

Loren watched Blair. He watched his brother sweat in the midmorning heat as he rode out twenty, twenty-five miles of Sundance's jarring trot. He looked back over his shoulder as he led the way down an unexpected drop in the terrain and saw the tenseness flash across Blair's face as Sundance dropped beneath him. From the corner of his eye Loren watched Blair maneuver through surprise attacks of tree branches brushing his face. "Branch," Loren would call, but not always in time.

He watched and waited, knowing Blair had never before stuck, for long, with difficult situations. He'd never had to. He probably wouldn't this time, and when he gave up, Loren would have clear sailing all the way to the junior division trophy of the Sangre Trek.

But the two weeks went by, and still Blair was there every morning, ready for the workout. Time to tighten the screws, Loren told himself.

Aloud he said, "Time to step up the training program, hermano." The family was sprawled in lawn chairs on the sloping side yard, digesting supper and enjoying the dry, cool evening air.

Blair, in the hammock, said, "Fine with me. What did you have in mind?"

Loren stared at him contemplatively. "Increase our riding time to four hours a day and start working steeper hills. The steepest we can find. And we should start teaching the horses a few of the fine points, too, like offside mounting and dismounting, since the book says you're never supposed to get on and off on the downhill side on a steep mountain trail. And Kade needs to get calmer about backing up. And we'll have to practice tailing."

The phone rang. Norma sighed and went to answer it.

"What's tailing?" Neal asked from behind *Newsweek*.

Before Loren could explain, Blair said, "That's when you get off your horse and drive him up a really steep place on the trail, rather than making him carry your

56

weight. You have a long rope attached to his halter, and you get behind him and hang onto the rope to steer him with, and you grab his tail and let him sort of pull you up."

Neal sniffed. "Sounds like a lot of monkey business to me. Horses are supposed to carry people, not haul them around with their tails. Aren't you likely to get kicked in the face?"

Blair laughed. "Not with good old Dancer. Loren might, though," he added cheerfully.

Loren scowled down toward his lap. He was surprised and mildly displeased that Blair remembered so much about tailing, just from having had the book read to him once. And he was more than a little uneasy about the prospect of tailing with Kade who was notoriously touchy about his hindquarters and having his back feet handled.

Norma emerged. "Blair, that was Alice Boldt, the woman from the Albuquerque newspaper, remember? She wants to come up tomorrow with her photographer and take some pictures of you and Sundance doing training-type things, you know, preparing for the Trek. She said they'll be here about nine in the morning. Let's see, I wonder if I've got a coffee cake in the freezer." She went back into the house to check.

Loren went to bed early and depressed. He lay there imagining the fun of having a picture story about himself and Kade in a Sunday paper that went all over the state. Mom would cut it out and keep it, and neighbors would bring over their extra copies so Mom could send them to out-of-state relatives. The girls at school . . .

He sighed and flopped over onto his back. Blair and I are doing the exact same identical thing, here. If anything, my part's harder. All he has to do is follow along after me. But who gets the glory? Blair, naturally. Blair is the big hero, just because he's blind.

I could be a hero, too. I know I could. But to be a hero you need the opportunity and, damn it, Blair's life is just one opportunity after another. But I could do it too, if I just had his advantages. Only nobody will ever know that.

He punched his pillow. I'll think of some way of stopping Blair. Maybe more pressure in the training. If that doesn't work I'll have to think of some way to sabotage his ride on the Trek. If it's the last thing I do, I'm going to come out on top, this once. Just this once.

Chapter 5

Blair lay in bed listening to "The Tonight Show." Pancho had been walking up and down the sheet that covered Blair but had finally come to rest near Blair's chin and had settled himself into a feather-fluff to sleep until Blair roused himself to take Pancho back to his cage.

Blair needed Pancho's company. His mind had long since ceased following the inane conversation of movie stars and had settled instead on his own problems.

Every muscle he owned still ached from this morning's ride even though hours had elapsed, even though the agony was less now than it had been two weeks ago. His arms and shoulders were as sore as his back and legs. The tension of balancing on Sundance was unrelenting, especially since Blair realized that Loren was trying to lure him into cantering and possibly laming Sundance with the strain of the gait. That had ended the ease of sitting in the saddle and being rocked along. Now the three hours must be spent balancing in his stirrups with most of his weight up off of Sundance's back. The book's dire warnings of saddle sores and back muscle damage from sitting a trot over long periods held Blair rigidly in place, but it was a killing position.

There was, too, the tension of needing always to be prepared for unexpected drops down or tilts up of the saddle beneath him, or for the changes in speed that Loren never announced but merely effected by changing Kade's gait and knowing Sundance would follow. And there was the startling unpleasantness of unexpected face-slaps by passing greenery. That situation was getting somewhat better now that Blair was learning to recognize, by an infinitesimal drop in the temperature of the air against his cheeks, when trees were near. He rode then with one forearm held up at an angle in front of his face to ward off branches, but the system wasn't a hundred percent, and more often than not a day's ride would add a scratch or two to his face.

But more unsettling than muscle aches or face scratches was the knowledge that Loren was somehow against him. In so many small ways, almost effortless ways, Loren could be making things easier for Blair. Before this Trek business had begun, Loren always called out change of terrain and speed when they rode together. It was habitual. Now Blair felt an attitude of "every man for himself" in Loren's leading of their training rides. Blair was uneasily aware of his dependence on Loren. All Loren would have to do would be to quit, to say he'd decided he didn't want to do the Trek. Blair would be up the creek without a paddle and left to look foolish in the eyes of everyone he knew.

A small hope stirred Blair into shifting positions, waking the bird on his clavicle.

If Lorey did pull out, then I wouldn't have to go through with it either, and I wouldn't be the one giving up. He'd be the quitter, not me.

The hope receded. Loren was a tough little buzzard, always had been.

I wish I had his guts.

The morning brought a brighter mood. Instead of doing their training ride, Blair and Loren hauled out the garden hose and shampooed both horses. It was a bright, hot morning and even in the early hours, cold water on bare legs and tennis shoes felt good. Kade fought the stream from the hose, but Sundance stood motionless while Blair sudsed along his mane and down his spine. Blair played the hose in Loren's direction and caught a flying wet sponge in the face, by way of retaliation. When the horses were finally rinsed and tied to the fence to dry, both boys were breathless from whooping and laughing.

Raven and Daisy Mae avoided the noise and the splashing water by staying in the far corner of the pasture.

By nine o'clock Blair and Loren were as cleaned and curried as the horses. They gathered in the piney living-room where Norma could watch out the front window for Alice Boldt and also for shop customers.

When the car with Albuquerque plates finally coasted to a stop near the house, Norma gave Blair a staccato description of the woman crossing the lawn toward the door.

"Youngish, skinny, frizzy hair, homely face, looks like she's got a sense of humor. Guy with her, must be the photographer, he's carrying cameras. Looks like a college kid. Beard. . . . Hi, come on in. You must be Miss Boldt, I'm Norma Liskey. Come right through here, watch the steps, this is my son Blair. And this is Loren, his brother."

Blair stood and extended his hand. "Hi."

"Blair," the woman said, and they all sat.

Voice sounded good, Blair thought, matter-of-fact and pleasant.

"This is my photographer, Jerry. I'd like to just ask you a few background questions first, Blair, and then maybe we can get some pictures outside with the horses. Okay?"

"Fire away." Blair could hear the photographer moving around the room. He wondered if the man was studying his face to find its best angles.

She began by asking his age, grade in school, names of all family members, hobbies and special interests.

"Girls," Loren offered. She grinned at him, but returned her attention to Blair.

Norma brought in coffee and coffee cake, then left when she saw a car stopping in front of the shop.

"Now, Blair," Miss Boldt said, "do you mind telling me a little about your condition?"

"Ten pounds overweight but otherwise prime." He grinned. "No, just kidding. I have retinitis pigmentosa. Want me to spell it?" She did. "I've had it from birth or at least infancy, it's an inherited defect that I received from my maternal grandmother. I have three percent vision and it is stable, that is, it will stay like this all my life. What else?"

His voice was bright.

She said, "Three percent vision. Can you describe what that looks like to you? Can you see me at all?"

"I can see a sort of a wavy blur in your general direction. It's hard for me to describe, since I've never seen any other way, but I'm told that it's something like looking down the wrong end of a telescope. It's all dark except for a small round area in the center of my field of vision, and in that I can see gross shapes, whoops, didn't mean to call you a gross shape"—they laughed—"and I can tell light from dark."

Blair heard Loren leave the room.

"How about color perception, depth perception?"

"Some color but I understand it's not at all accurate, and no usable depth perception since I can't see objects clearly enough for that." He wondered for an instant where Loren had gone, but he was having too much fun to care.

After a few general questions about the Sangre Trek, Miss Boldt stood. "Why don't we go outside now, and get some shots with the horses. Tell me, what made you want to take on something like this?" she asked as they moved toward the back door.

Blair shrugged. "The challenge, I guess. There are so few ways that I can compete with other people on anything like an equal basis, and this is one way that I can, since the horse can do the navigating, to some extent."

"And your brother."

"Oh, absolutely. I couldn't do it without him."

Loren was waiting for them at the corral. Blair located Sundance and found the saddle and bridle already in place. He gritted back his irritation. He'd gotten so smooth at the saddling operation, and it would have made a good shot.

He heard a soft click-whirr behind and to the left. It was repeated from a different angle. The camera, he thought, and sucked in his stomach.

Jerry took charge. "Let's bring the horse over here, away from that background clutter. There, that's good. Now, if you'd get on him, ride him around a little."

Blair led Sundance away from the shed, turned until the sun was in his face, then mounted.

Miss Boldt called, "Can you push your hat back a little? We're getting shadows on your face. That's good."

Blair rode in easy loping circles and figure eights while the camera click-whirred. He felt charged with the excitement of the moment. Except for the morning they had rated the horses, Blair had never before ridden when he was not following another rider. Power and exhilaration washed over him, so that he almost forgot the photographer. Beneath him was the solid familiarity of Sundance, whose shape and movement and dependability were becoming almost a part of Blair's own body, an extension of himself but an extension that could see. These past weeks of intensive riding had done more to create this bond than the previous two years of occasional rides had.

"Okay, that's enough," Jerry called, and Blair aimed Sundance toward the voice.

Jerry said, "Do some on-the-ground things, you know, unsaddling, whatever you'd do after a training session. Loren, let's have you doing something in the background."

Blair heard Loren and Kade coming into camera range.

Blair located the corral fence and tied his reins to it, then pulled off the saddle, heaved it atop the fence, and spread the saddle blanket over it to dry. Click-whirr, click-whirr.

He offered Sundance a drink from a bucket of water supplied by Loren. Click-whirr.

He knelt beside Sundance's near foreleg, locked his fingers together behind the cannon bone, and began to massage the sides of the horse's legs with the heels of his hands, pushing upward toward the heart with every stroke, as the book had instructed. With the flat of his hand he massaged the bulge of muscle in Dance's upper leg, still pushing up toward the heart. He worked his hands down the length of the horse's spine on either side of the bone, and ended with a gentle squeezing motion along the ridge of Sundance's neck. Click-whirr.

As Miss Boldt and the photographer began moving toward their car, Blair wanted, suddenly, to tell her how he'd felt while he was riding, to make her understand the sudden exhilaration of moving fast, alone and virtually under his own power, with no fear of crashing into something, or falling. He wanted her to understand the unexpected rush of love he'd felt for Sundance at that moment, the feeling of becoming a centaur.

But for once his glib tongue failed him.

It seemed to Blair that after that day Loren grew less communicative, except for their work with the horses. He heard his brother doing push-ups in his room early every morning, but Loren never suggested that Blair should be exercising, too. And when they came back from their rides and went to the refrigerator, Blair no longer heard the customary snap-fizz of Loren's pop cans. Loren was obviously drinking fruit juice or milk. Blair, too, began doing push-ups and drinking fruit juice instead of pop, but nothing was said, by either of them, and Blair was uneasy.

The days passed, and Loren increased their riding time by gradual stages, as the horses toughened. At the end of the third week they were riding three hours in the mornings and another two after lunch, and holding the horses to a pace that was gradually increasing.

One morning Loren said, "Our training time is about half gone now. I'd say we're coming along pretty good. What we need more of now is practice on steep places, leading and tailing, and stuff like that."

An uneasy prickle went through Blair. Trotting along on flatlands or low hills was one thing. Scrambling around steep mountainsides was something he'd avoided thinking about as much as possible.

"Right," he said firmly.

They rode for some distance across Kenns' pasture, then halted.

Loren said, "Okay, we're going to leave the trail and go straight up this hill. First we'll do it mounted, then we'll practice tailing."

"How high up are we going," Blair asked, "and what kind of an angle have we got?"

"I'm not going to tell you that. I won't have time to explain every little up and down on the Trek, so you may as well get used to it. Remember to stand in your stirrups going up, and get your weight forward and give him his head so he can work. I'll go first, you give me a little lead and then follow. It'll be safer if the horses aren't too close together."

Blair felt himself go pale.

Kade scrambled away. Blair held Sundance back for just a second, then gave him his head. Beneath him he felt the horse tilt upward sharply, and for a sickening instant Blair and the horse seemed to be toppling forward out of control.

He clenched against the fear and concentrated on balancing over the lurching body beneath him. Lunge by lunge they climbed, until Sundance came to a halt near the sound of Kade's breathing. A trembling began in Blair's legs.

"Okay, now we'll go back down," Loren said brightly. "Remember to lean back and brace against your stirrups, or you'll fall off over his head. This hill is just about straight up and down here. Give him his head, he'll need to use it to keep his balance. You go first this time, and I'll follow."

Blair fought back an urge to whimper as the saddle tilted and Sundance began a stiff-legged, hopping, sliding descent. Blair leaned back, braced his feet, and prayed. Close behind him came the scrambling sound of Kade and Loren, pressing too close, pushing Sundance too fast.

But before he could pull in enough breath to snarl at Loren, the descent was over and they were on the level again. He heard Loren dismount.

"Now we'll practice tailing."

Wearily Blair nodded, and stepped down. This was bound to be easier.

Loren said, with a note of sarcasm, "As you know from reading my book, we'll need to tail up some of the really steep places, to save wear and tear on the horses. You remember how the book said to do it? Okay, I'll go first so all Sundance will have to do is follow. I might have some trouble controlling Kade, so be ready to jump out of the way if I yell. Take your position."

Blair looped his reins around the saddle horn, leaving enough slack for Sundance to get his head down. He snapped onto Sundance's halter the long rope brought for this purpose, and ran the rope back through his stirrup.

Then he moved back and got a solid double handful of the horse's tail. He felt the curving of Sundance's body as the horse turned to look at him.

Loren clucked to Kade, yelled whoa, straightened him out, and clucked him forward again. Blair said, "Go, boy," and Sundance moved forward.

Up the hill they went. With his feet on firm ground and Sundance's tail and rope to pull him along, Blair found the climb surprisingly easy. The slope was much less severe than Loren had described it, Blair could tell.

He was trying to psych me out, he thought. Anger flared, but there was no time to explore the thought.

At the top, Loren said, "Good. That worked out slicker than sweat. Now let's try leading them downhill. The book said the winning riders usually get off and lead, going down really steep places, and they do it at a pretty fast clip. You go first."

Blair was still puffing from the climb, but he unwound his reins from the saddle horn and started down the slope with Sundance at his shoulder.

"Faster," Loren called.

Blair tried to increase his speed. He stepped on a loose rock, his foot twisted and he fell, catching himself on hands and knees, but not before Sundance's hoof grazed his hip. Another hoof mashed Blair's booted toe into the earth.

"You okay?" Loren called cheerfully.

"Yeah." Blair climbed to his feet and hobbled on down the slope, more shaken by the fall than he would admit, even to himself.

When they were both mounted and riding again, it seemed to Blair that Sundance was favoring one front leg, just a shade. But after a few steps the irregularity, if it had existed, disappeared and Blair had time to think about Loren, to wonder at the hostility that had crept into Loren's training program.

After the ride, during the liniment rub that was now part of the daily routine, it seemed to Blair that the lower part of Sundance's near foreleg was a little warmer than the other legs. Or was it? He couldn't be sure.

"That's a bowed tendon," the vet said. "No question about it. This flexor tendon along the back of the leg here—see, where the swelling is—that tendon has been pulled or strained in some way. He'll be all right eventually, but he'll need cold packs twice a day till the swelling goes down, and then complete rest for at least, oh, three months anyway."

It was Saturday, and the whole family was at the lunch table. The vet's truck had just driven away.

"I can't believe it," Norma said. "Of all the horses we've got, Sundance is the only solid rock, the one you don't expect something like this to happen to."

"A darned shame," Neal said. "I know how much you boys were looking forward to the Trek, and you've both worked so hard, training for it. And that newspaper article, I suppose they'll have to scrap it now."

Loren said, "According to the book, approximately half of the horses who begin training for a distance ride don't make it through the training, or get vetted out at the beginning of the ride. That means they don't pass the initial vet check. So, even though it's tough luck for Blair, we are right in there with the averages."

Norma said, "Loren."

"Well? It's true."

"You don't need to sound so chipper about it. Blair's worked just as hard as you have to get ready for the Trek. You might be a little considerate of his feelings."

Blair was silent, but his mind raced. Sundance out of the running. The perfect out for me. With no horse I can't be expected to go on with it. No more training. I won't have to scramble around those mountains. I won't have to trust Loren to get me through it safely.

Loren. He's so happy about this he can hardly hold it in. I can hear it in his voice, if nobody else can. He was hoping for something like this. Why? Does he hate me? Why would he care if I went on the Trek or not? What's it to him? He's already got everything. Is he jealous about the newspaper story?

But he was in no mood for philosophy and understanding. He wanted to hit out at Loren, to defend himself against his enemy.

Blair cleared his throat, and the others stopped talking about refunds of entry fees. "You're forgetting something. It's just the horse that's out of the game, not the rider. We've got other horses."

"Raven?" Norma said, her voice rising to a squeak.

Blair nodded.

Loren exploded. "You can't ride him on the Trek. He hardly ever gets ridden. He's completely out of condition, and the ride's only five weeks away. He'd never catch up in time, and I'll be darned if I'm going to hold Kade back. It was bad enough with Sundance. I was always having to hold back so he could keep up, and I would have never had a chance to win the Trek at that rate.

And now, if we have to start all over again with Raven, it'll be that much worse."

Norma regained her voice. "I don't know. Now that I think about it—Raven doesn't get much riding, but he's running in the pasture all the time, so he's probably not in too bad shape. He's got good feet, and he's not as fat as Sundance was when you started his conditioning. I think it's worth a try, anyway."

Blair said, "Tell you what, Lor. I'll take Raven along on the morning rides, and you can go alone in the afternoons, at least for the first few days till he starts toughening up. If he can't hack it, then I won't do the ride, but if he can—"

Loren was cornered, and Blair knew it. Blair smiled and tried not to think about what he had just let himself in for.

Chapter 6

Loren leaned back against a sun-warmed rock and stared into the far distance, the gray-green landscape rippling away to the east below him. His eyes were tired after three hours of studying the near ground in front of Kade as it unrolled at ten miles an hour. Rattlesnakes and prairie dog holes had a way of appearing in the worst places if you didn't watch out for them.

In one hand he held a single-serving can of V-8, and in the other the remaining corner of a peanut butter sandwich. It was only nine-thirty, but on training rides the lunch break came early and felt well earned. Just behind him, Blair lay flat out on his back, straw hat propped over his face. Kade and Raven cropped at whatever grass they could reach in the radius of their halter ropes. Their bare backs showed squares of sweat where the saddles were, with streaks of sweat-mud trickling down toward their flanks.

Loren pulled the little notebook from his pocket and studied its figures. After five weeks of training Kade's readings showed a definite improvement. Although they were still higher than the averages listed in the book, both pulse and respiration rates now dropped to near-normal, well within the fifteen-minute time limit the Trek judges would be using. He was going to be fine.

Raven, after two weeks, was showing a marked improvement in his readings also, but with some puzzling patterns. Several times he had gone into inversion, with respiration faster than pulse. Loren still didn't understand exactly why this was dangerous—the book hadn't been specific on that point—but he did know that an inverted reading during the Trek would mean instant elimination from further competition. It was a hope, he reminded himself. But it was also a puzzle. He scowled as he tried to figure out a pattern to the inversions. They seemed to happen most often during the first hour of the training ride, but not always. And, he noted, they were happening less frequently this week than last week. It was probably nothing.

Loren was mildly surprisd to find himself relieved at the thought. He glanced back over his shoulder at his dozing brother. Blair had guts all right, Loren reflected. That first week with Raven couldn't have been easy. The rusty black had been irate at the idea of long daily rides taking him away from his pasture and Daisy. He'd been hard to catch, he'd gritted his teeth against the invasion of the bit in his mouth, and he'd proved a master at blowing himself up at cinch-tightening time, then releasing his breath as Blair mounted so that the saddle slipped and the riding was delayed.

Once underway Raven had alternated between sulking along well behind Kade and wanting to crowd past the chestnut into the lead. Kade didn't like Raven and he didn't like being bumped from the rear, and once, before Loren could stop him, Kade had lashed out with both hind hooves and caught Blair a nasty crack on the shin. Blair had paled momentarily, then made a weak joke and ridden on.

By the second week of Raven's training things began to smooth out. The horse grew accustomed to the routine and went along much more willingly, even seeming to enjoy the work as the initial ache of unused muscles gradually disappeared.

"You know what we need to do now," Loren said suddenly.

Blair grunted.

"We need to—are you awake?—we need to get these horses out of this old familiar pasture and into a group of strange horses. We need to get Raven used to going in close quarters with other horses. Kade should be okay, he's been on enough Saddle Club trail rides, but Raven hasn't, and he can be kind of undependable around other horses. If he's going to cause trouble, we better find out about it before the Trek, right?"

Blair hesitated before he said, firmly, "Good idea. Shall we call Bill Don and see if there are any Saddle Club rides coming up? They have them about every other weekend, don't they?"

The next Sunday morning three horses trotted along the edge of the highway toward Rebano, an arch-necked liver-chestnut Arabian, a rangy black, and a stocky little pinto pony who bore a grinning woman rider.

"Hey, you guys," Norma called. "Let's walk a while. You may be toughened up to this, but remember your gray-haired old mother back here. I'm getting blisters already."

74

Neal drove past slowly in the pickup with a cooler full of potato salad and soft drinks in the back. He grinned and waved at the riders from the comfort of his truck seat, which was just where he wanted to be.

The ride was already gathering in the weedy little recreation park at the edge of town. Two dozen riders, many of them children younger than Blair and Loren, milled around the parked trailers and stock trucks, while several women worked around a long picnic table, setting out potluck offerings.

The membership of the club comprised, informally, whatever Rebano area families were currently interested enough in trail riding to get together on alternate Sundays throughout the summer for an afternoon of eating and riding. There was an annual business meeting and chili supper in January, the business meeting usually lasting no more than ten minutes and offering members only flashes of time to present new and old business before getting on to the chili.

During the first year that the Liskeys had horses, the entire family had gone on one trail ride. But Neal and Raven didn't get along, Neal didn't enjoy the ride, and for the remainder of that season only Norma and the boys had ridden with the club. The second year the three of them had gone only once or twice, this year not at all, so far. Loren and Blair had been too intent on racking up their training mileage, and Norma only went to enjoy watching her sons having a good time.

As the Liskeys rode into the park, a large, beefy Navajo came toward them, leading a bony bay gelding. He grinned at Norma and Loren as the three dismounted, then he reached toward Blair and jammed down the brim of Blair's hat. "Glad y'all could make it. We been missing you on our rides this year."

Blair and Bill Don exchanged arm punches. Loren watched. Norma fell into step beside the man as they led the horses toward the picket line to tie them during lunch. She said, "When is your grandfather going to have another sand painting for me? I think I may have a buyer for the big one."

Bill Don acted as agent for his grandfather, who created the exquisite sand paintings in Norma's shop, building landscapes of tans and whites and turquoise, a grain at a time, in glass frames. They were expensive and sold slowly, but Norma loved them.

Loren tied Kade on the line well away from Raven in case they should start kicking, then pulled off his saddle and bridle and rubbed the corners of Kade's mouth where the bit always seemed to make him itchy. He held his hands still for an instant, and Kade nodded his head between Loren's palms until the itching was eased. Loren grinned. His eyes followed the lines of Kade's body, the neatly arched neck, the sleek narrow but deep barrel, the high tail set. Looking down the row of miscellaneous mounts tied to the picket line, Loren suddenly felt a sense of rightness about being coupled with Kade. Bill Don's huge bay matched the man; Daisy May was little and sweet and dependable, like Mom; Raven, well, Raven didn't count. Substitute Sundance and you'd have a nice big old wise horse that never did anything wrong, like Blair. Mrs. Elsing's horse was as gray-haired as she was, the two little Miller kids rode matching pinto shetlands, and so on down the line. The matching up didn't always come out right, but Loren realized that even when horse and rider bore no outward resemblance there was usually a similarity of character traits.

He rested his eyes again on Kade and felt good.

The potluck lunch was ample and good, but Loren ate little and so, he noticed, did Blair. Loren tried to put himself in Blair's place at this moment but it wasn't a pleasant prospect, riding Raven for four hours in this crowd of strange horses. Probably he'd be okay, Loren told himself. It was just the fear of the unknown. At least he had only Kade to worry about and Kade was, if not perfect, at least familiar.

Paper plates disappeared into garbage containers and the saddling up began. Loren glanced at Blair as his brother located his saddle and heaved it up onto Raven's back. Blair's face had that tight, colorless look that Loren was beginning to recognize as fear.

Why don't you give it up? Loren thought. You don't have to be doing this. You don't need to prove anything, everyone already thinks you're wonderful.

The ride mounted and moved out, twenty-three horses and ponies jogging across the park and onto an abandoned railroad right-of-way that bore horse tracks all summer and snowmobile tracks all winter. It was a pleasant trail a dozen feet wide, raised above the surrounding land, and shaded by weedy young trees that had grown up since the cessation of train traffic. Loren began to relax and enjoy himself. He'd forgotten how slow a pace these trail rides set, compared to what he and Blair were used to.

He turned and called back over his shoulder to Blair, "This is going to be a piece of cake, hermano."

Blair smiled back and waved the end of his reins in salute. Just at that moment the two Miller children sent

77

their ponies charging past the line of horses in a screeching attempt to catch up with someone at the head of the line. Kade shied, nearly stumbling off the edge of the right-of-way, and Loren heard Raven snorting and crashing through brush. By the time Loren was able to look, Blair had Raven straightened out and going again, but the set, gray look was back on Blair's face.

"Darned kids, anyway," Norma called from behind Blair. "Somebody ought to beat some trail manners into those two, on the seat of their pants. Are you okay, Blair?"

"Sure."

Loren's PRs returned to normal.

After a few miles the ride left the railroad trail and filed through a gate onto pastureland belonging to one of the Saddle Club members. It was rolling open grassland, and the riders fanned out and formed conversational groups. Bill Don dropped back beside Blair.

"Say, I was sure sorry to hear about your buckskin going lame on you. He's a nice horse. He going to be okay, is he?"

Blair said, "Yeah, he's coming along fine. Had to cold-pack him for a while there, was all."

"Will you be able to use him on your big ride then?"

Blair shook his head. "No, but I've been working Raven, here, and I think he's going to be in shape in time."

Bill Don shook his head. "Gotta hand it to you, kid. I don't think I'd do it, if I was in your place. Hell, I'm not even doing it in *my* place. A hundred miles through those mountains, whew." He shook his head again.

The horses ahead disappeared over the lip of a gulley. When Loren sent Kade sliding down the descent he saw at the bottom a shallow stream a few yards wide, a foot or so deep, its mossy rock bed showing through the clear water.

Water crossings, Loren thought suddenly. *That's* what we haven't practiced on our training rides.

A few horses were in the water, drinking. Loren held his breath and urged Kade forward with his legs. The chestnut curved his neck and stiffened his ears. His body tensed but with only a token hesitation Kade stepped into the water, picked his way to the middle, then dropped his head for a drink. Loren breathed again, and turned to watch Raven's crossing.

Daisy Mae and Bill Don's horse waded in. Raven balked at the edge of the water. Blair kicked and rein-slapped, but Raven only flattened his ears and backed away.

"Pop him a good one," Loren yelled.

Blair managed to drive the horse to the edge of the water again, but there Raven dug his hooves into the gravel and balked. Blair's face reddened as he flailed Raven's flanks with his rein-ends.

Two riders descended the slope behind Raven and crowded past into the water. Raven lashed at one of them with his heels and spun away from the water once again.

In a worried voice Norma said, "Honey, maybe you should try getting off and leading him through. The water's only a few inches deep."

But Blair only muttered something through clenched teeth and went on turning Raven toward the water again and again and whomping at him with his reins. Loren became aware that the rest of the ride was leaving them behind.

"Here, I'll help you," Bill Don said. He rode up fast and hard behind Raven and cracked the black rump with his rawhide quirt.

Raven leaped.

Blair, caught off balance, toppled. He landed on his back in the water just as Raven made a splash landing in midstream, then, with another mighty bound, surged out of the stream and plunged up the far bank. Instinctively Loren sent Kade after the horse, made a lucky grab, and caught the reins. He turned and looked back.

Blair was sitting up in the water, half-supported by Norma and Bill Don. He shook his head as though he was dazed.

"You okay?" Loren called.

In answer, Blair climbed to his feet and sent a grin in Loren's direction. "The old crow got his revenge on me, that's for sure. Did you catch him?" The party waded across, Blair reaching toward Loren, Norma and Bill Don following with arms stretched in mute support, Daisy Mae and the bay trailing and snatching final sips of water.

"I think we ought to go back," Norma said. "You took quite a fall there. Did you hit your head at all? Do you have any dizziness or nausea?"

"Oh, Mom. I just had a nice little bath, that's all." Blair felt his way along Raven to the stirrup, and mounted.

But Loren saw his brother's face, and he had a sudden sense of what it cost Blair to step up into that saddle.

Press your advantage, Loren told himself. He's weak now, maybe he'll crack.

He maneuvered Kade beside Raven and said, "Well, we learned one thing already today, hermano. We're going to have to work that buzzard over every water crossing we can find. I expect we'll have lots worse water crossings than that one on the Trek, and he's going to have to go through them without fussing, or it could really be dangerous."

Blair said softly, "Sure wish I had old Sundance back." Then, in a stronger voice, "We could do our training rides over this way for a few days till we get him going across that creek like he's supposed to, and then maybe we can find some other places to practice with him."

Loren just sighed.

Loren lay awake, hands locked behind his head, eyes staring up at nothing. At the problem. Blair had emerged from the bathroom earlier that evening wearing just his shower towel and showing huge purpling bruises on his back from the rocks in the stream bed. He was limping slightly on one leg and taking, Loren thought, shallower breaths than normal, as though his ribs hurt.

Why doesn't he give up? Loren wailed silently. He didn't *want* to admire Blair's guts. He wanted to hate them.

Only three more weeks till the Trek, he thought. It looks like Raven's going to be in at least pretty good condition by that time, and I guess it's obvious by now that Blair's not going to chicken out. So where does that leave me and Kade? Bringing up the end of the line with Blair.

Maybe Raven will be fast enough to make good time. He does move along faster than Sundance. When he wants to.

Yes, but he's not going to be in as good shape as he should be, not even with three more weeks of training.

We'll have to go at an easy speed or his PRs are going to shoot right through the roof.

Well? Wouldn't that be an out? If his readings are over seventy/forty after the rest periods, or if he goes into an inversion, the judges will pull him and I'll be free to go on at my own speed.

Loren pondered, then the argument resumed. Yes, but that would be dangerous to Raven. He may not be my favorite horse in the world but I sure don't want him going into a heart attack or colic, or something like that that he could die from, just for the sake of me winning the trophy. And besides, in another three weeks Raven might be shaped up enough that his readings won't be going so high. He's making progress faster than Sundance did. So I better be thinking up something else, a Plan B in case both Blair and Raven are still hanging in there, say, by the second day of the race.

Loren squeezed his eyes shut and tried to picture the ride. He knew from studying the information mailed to him by the Sangre Trek Committee that the riders would be released at thirty-second intervals, each rider being timed out and timed back in again at the end of each day's ride. The winner in each division, heavyweight, light-weight, novice, and junior, would be the horse and rider completing the ride in the shortest actual riding time providing that the horse passed its final vet check and was pro-nounced sound at the end of the ride.

So there'll be no advantage in starting off at the head of the group, Loren thought. What if we requested the two last positions, so that the rest of the junior division would be up ahead of us and only the drag riders behind us. Okay. Then, let's see. What if Blair and I got off the trail, just a little ways, till the drag riders got past. Then I could lose Blair, get back on the trail, make up the time . . .

No. I couldn't come riding in without Blair. And he'd know what I was doing. He'd be as mad as hell. He'd tell everybody that I did it on purpose, and that would make me the real villain, man. Dumping my blind brother out on some mountain trail.

I'd have to make Blair believe it was an accident some-how. And I'd have to think of something believable to tell the drag riders when I caught up with them. Still, if worst comes to worst and I have to go to Plan B, I bet I could pull it off. And he won't be in any real danger, or anything like that. All he'll have to do when he realizes we got separated is just give Raven his head. Any horse with any sense will follow the trail the other horses have been on. He'll come in okay, he'll just be slower. And if I can get Kade away from him long enough to make up some time . . .

Chapter 7

"Come back and to the right, about five inches, whoa, go forward again."

Loren stood in front of the horse trailer and stared intently at the approach of the hitch ball on the back of the pickup.

Neal, at the wheel of the truck, called, "Am I straight?" and the truck eased back.

"Almost, almost, easy, whoa! I think we can get it now." Loren kneeled on the neck of the trailer and rocked it to the left. Neal came around and added his weight, and together they forced the trailer's socket over the hitch ball. The latch closed, the catch sleeve eased forward, and the hitch was secured.

"Whew." Loren and Neal straightened and shook hands.

Neal said, "Why don't you start loading the horses, and I'll get started on the gear."

Norma stood in the yard near the breezeway, pointing to the piles around her and reciting from her list. "Tent, tent poles, tent stakes, and hammer," she said with special emphasis, remembering the camping trip when she had been responsible for forgetting the stakes and had been lectured by Neal all weekend. "Boys' suitcase, our suitcase. Knee bandages, cinch covers, horse blankets. Extra saddle blankets. Extra saddle blankets," she yelled, and Loren answered, "Under the saddles."

She nodded. "Water buckets, sponges, brushes, two hoof picks. Right. Got 'em. Oats. Oats? Here they are. Hay, two bales, in the truck already. What am I forgetting? I'm forgetting something."

Loren came through, leading El Kadir. The horse was gleaming, his hide polished by six weeks of serious grooming and the increased grain in his diet. At the rear of the trailer he shied and fussed and tried to swing away, but it was only a token resistance. He gathered himself and leaped in, and before Loren had finished tying his lead rope, he was at work on the net full of hay that hung before him.

Neal began loading tent, tack, and gear into the back of the pickup. Blair sat in the car, waiting.

Through the breezeway Loren came leading the rangy rusty black. Raven, too, looked better than his everyday self. His mane lay neatly, his shaggy fetlocks had been scissored to a semblance of neatness, and his white hind foot was shampooed clean. His coat, like Kade's, glowed from brushing. He looked, if not handsome, at least presentable.

Raven stepped calmly into the trailer. As Loren jumped out and closed the doors he thought, Wouldn't it be ironic if Raven turned out to be a better trail horse than Sundance? Or Kade?

A crooked smile twisted his lips, and he reached over the tailgate door to pat the maroon-brown hips. Eight weeks of intensive riding with Kade had given Loren a feeling of partnership with the horse that was unexpected and in an odd way exciting. Kade had developed the habit of cocking one ear back toward Loren's voice at moments when he wasn't sure of himself, to listen for Loren's encouragement or praise or corrections. And more and more frequently Kade was beginning to change his gait just as Loren was thinking of making the change.

Kade still bucked going into a canter, and there were still times when he and Loren parted company, but in Loren's mind the bucking began to take on the aspects of a contest, an arm-wrestle between best friends. Sometimes he won, sometimes Kade did, but the element of equality between them created a mutual respect, a kindling affection.

During these past few weeks while Loren and Blair had repeatedly forced Raven back and forth across whatever water they could find, from creeks to mud puddles, Loren had come to recognize and admire his horse's courage. Kade might shy at a sudden movement, a bird or rabbit coming up under his feet, or even the sight of a suspicious log lying close beside the trail. But Loren began to perceive Kade's reactions as a finely honed instinct for self-preservation, rather than as a lack of courage. The log might have been a bear, after all, and if it had, Kade's instant evasion might have made the difference between life and death.

But in contrast with Raven, Kade's courage was beautiful to Loren. Raven was close-minded, self-serving. If he decided he didn't want to go into water it took all of the boys' skill, diligence, and sometimes anger to move him. Kade seemed willing to take Loren's word that it was safe to go ahead and seldom hesitated more than an instant, no matter what the strange water crossing or tricky terrain might look like.

Loren looked at Kade's courage, like Blair's, as a quality to be admired above all others, but Kade's courage belonged to Loren, was on Loren's side of the battle; he could take pride in it rather than having to envy it as he did Blair's. And Blair's courage became more and more apparent in those weeks after Blair's accident ⊙n the trail ride. His brother seemed to be continually pushing Loren to find more water crossings, more challenges for Raven.

Gradually, over those three weeks, Loren gave up hope of Blair's backing out of the Trek. He obviously wasn't being scared off by the switch from Sundance to Raven, and although the black horse was frequently mule-headed he had muscled up sufficiently by now so that there was no good reason not to take him on the Trek. His readings occasionally inverted but only for a short time, and his sweat had changed from the sudsy foam of a soft horse to the clear, watery sweat of a horse in prime condition.

But Raven was slow. After two or three hours of riding he would begin to lag and Blair was afraid to push the horse too hard, knowing that he wasn't completely hardened yet for maximum effort. Training rides ended with Kade still full of prance and Loren full of frustration. He wanted to drive himself and Kadir to the limits of their strength, to see where those limits were. And he wanted to be free of the drag of Raven and Blair, free from the necessity of taking care of them.

The bitterness that had been growing in Loren all summer was coming to a head. He could feel it. He didn't understand the force within him that made him need to stop Blair, but he felt, instinctively, that if Blair came through this ride smelling like a rose, getting fame and attention from that damned newspaper article, then Loren Liskey was forever going to be the invisible brother. Nothing he could ever accomplish would make him Blair's equal.

He knew he would never have had the guts to do what Blair had been doing all summer, even on Sundance, much less on Raven. To ride without being able to see where you were going. He shivered when he thought of it. He knew his own fears about smaller challenges than that and he knew, he *knew* Blair was the better man.

The Trek was going to prove it. If Blair had backed out when Sundance was hurt, nobody would have held it against him. Then Loren and El Kadir would have gone on to glory, unhampered by Blair's slowness, by the constant, oh God, the *constant* need to hold back his own progress to help Blair along. Loren and El Kadir would have had a shot at the junior division trophy, some glory of their own.

But Blair was still on Loren's back. He sat there in that car, smugly waiting for the work to be done so they could get going.

I'll have to stop him, Loren thought. Or at least beat him.

The truck and trailer coasted through Rebano and began climbing into the mountains, going in second gear much of the way. Neal drove and Loren rode silently beside him, while the car followed with Norma and Blair.

Neal said, "You've got your entry information, and your map of the ride, and all that?"

"Yo."

"Lorey, you'll watch out for Blair, won't you?"

Loren scowled and snapped, "Don't I always?"

"Sure, but this is a pretty big challenge for him. I want you to promise that you won't take any dumb chances. Winning is not important. Even finishing the ride, that's not important. What is, is that Blair has this as a positive experience. You know what I mean? It will do him a world of good, just coming through this ride. He needs to build self-confidence, and this could be so good for him."

"He's got plenty of self-confidence," Loren muttered out the window.

"He talks a good game, Lorey, but I think he feels pretty shaky sometimes about leaving home, going to college, out into the world. You know. So let's see to it that this ride is a positive experience for him, okay?"

"How about me? I could use a positive experience once in a while myself. Did anybody ever think about that?"

Neal gave him a gentle look, but didn't bother to answer. Blair's blindness was too obvious, between them, to need mentioning.

The gathering place for the Sangre Trek was a rodeo ground just outside of Majestad, a small town high in the Sangre de Christo range. Although the town fell considerably short of its name it was a pleasant place full of Old West atmosphere and pine-washed air. Motels with names like The Silver Spur lined the little highway on either end of Majestad and souvenir shops made up most of the downtown area, but the touristy aspects of the town seemed to project a sense of fun, as though hosts and guests were involved together in an ongoing game of cowboys and Indians.

Almost in spite of himself Loren grew excited as they drove through Majestad. Just ahead of them was a dusty horse trailer bearing a sign that read, "Majestad or bust." The licence plates said West Virginia. Across the main street hung a huge banner saying, "Welcome Eighth Annual Sangre Trek." Loren swelled with the feeling of being part of something big.

Beyond the last of the motels they turned, at an arrow marked "Trekkies," onto a small dirt road that took them to the rodeo grounds. Near the entrance gate a woman approached them, grinning. She was big-boned and brown, with a long black braid down her back and a clipboard in her arms.

"Welcome to the Trek," she said. "I'm Karen Crow, ride chairman. Your name is?"

Loren spoke across his father. "Loren Liskey, and my brother Blair is in the car behind us."

Neal said, proudly, "My wife and I are the ground crew."

"Fine. We need plenty of those." She made two checks on her clipboard papers. "Loren, your stall number is fourteen, and Blair's is fifteen. Stables are over there, those gray buildings beyond the bleachers. You'll be camping on the grounds?" She glanced at the gear in the pickup. "You can set up anyplace from the stables on back. You'll find some other campers already set up there. At five o'clock there'll be a barbecue dinner for all participants, courtesy of the town, and at seven we'll all meet at the bleachers for our briefing. That's very important, so don't miss it.

When you get unloaded, check at the registration table for your credentials. Welcome to the Trek, have a marvelous time, and good luck on the ride."

They drove across a grassy meadow surrounded by pine-forested slopes. It was a lovely natural amphitheater, a fitting stage for rodeo spectacles and endurance rides. At the center was a fenced oval with stock chutes at one end, a raised judges' stand, and bleachers along the sides. Beyond the arena was a grid of square corrals with iron pipe fences for rodeo stock.

The stables were long, narrow sheds made of grayed wood shingles, four buildings that sprawled beneath giant pines. Numbers were painted in runny green paint above the Dutch doors of the stalls.

"Fourteen and fifteen," Loren said.

A deeply weathered little man with brilliant silver hair appeared beside Loren's window.

"Howdee there, welcome to the Trek. I'm stable boss, so anything you need, you let me know. You got your stall number?"

"Fourteen and fifteen," Loren said.

"You're there already. Just down the end of this row here. There's a bale of straw in each stall and plenty more when you need it. Down thataway there you'll find pitch-forks and wheelbarrows and extra bedding, if you need hay or oats let me know, and there's water faucets all along there, see 'em? Glad you could make it, good luck on the ride."

Loren and Norma spread the straw in the two stalls, while Neal filled the horses' water buckets and hung them in the stalls. Wary of last minute injuries, Loren backed

Kade and Raven out of the trailer and turned them into their stalls. Then truck, trailer, and car snaked through the trees to the camping area.

They chose a spot near the restroom building, for Blair's convenience, and spread the awkward bulk of stiff khaki canvas tent between them, one Liskey at each corner.

"Back and to the left, Blair," Norma said. "You've got wrinkles. There, that's pretty good."

With only minimal difficulties the structure rose and was made secure on its frame of interlocking aluminum tubes and guy ropes. It was furnished with air mattresses and sleeping bags, suitcase and ice chest and battery lamp.

They drove back to town to eat lunch and check in at Neal and Norma's motel, then returned to the rodeo grounds.

"I believe we'll leave you boys here," Norma said brightly, as they drew up before the tent, "and go do some sight-seeing. I think your barbecue dinner is supposed to be just for riders, not ground crew, so we'll get something in town and check in with you later in the evening. Okay? You got everything you need?"

"Yes," Loren and Blair said together.

"If you need us for anything, you know where we are. Have fun."

As the car disappeared, Loren grew tense, charged with nervous energy. Hours to kill before the dinner and briefing. Hours to try not to think about tomorrow.

Blair was settled, apparently calmly, in one of the folding lawn chairs in front of the tent.

Sitting there smiling, Loren thought. Waiting for me to lead him around by the hand and do most of the work while he plays it to the hilt, brave blind boy challenging the mountain. If he wasn't here and I was doing this alone—

"Hey, Lor, shouldn't we be doing something?"

Loren sighed. "Yeah. Let's go check in at the registration table. You want the restrooms?"

"No, but where are they?"

"To the right about ten yards, and the door is around the corner of the building, to the right."

They walked out from under the trees into the sunlight, and in spite of his brother Loren felt exhilarated. People wandered across the grass, smiling when they met his gaze, or talking to one another over maps and lists. Excitement seemed to generate from each jeaned and booted figure. Horses were led or ridden across the meadow in a slow-motion crisscross, their heads hanging easy.

A small cluster of riders stood near the long table behind the judge's stand, where smiling, sunbrowned women sat dispensing information. Loren steered toward what appeared to be the end of the line and prepared to wait.

The tee-shirted figure in front of him caught his attention. Small, feminine, nicely rounded. Short tan curls showed around the bottom of a billed cap covered with souvenir buttons.

"Hi," he said quickly, before there was time to lose his nerve. "My name's Loren Liskey."

She turned, flicked him with her gaze, and held out her hand. "Hi. Sandy Fields. No jokes please. Where you from?"

She had a nice, open, freckled face and big gray-green eyes, and a mouth that curled up at the corners. Sixteen, seventeen, Loren figured. He liked her instantly.

"I'm from here," he said. "Well, Rebano, about sixty miles east of here. You?"

"Bismarck. North Dakota."

"Wow, that's a long way. Who'd you come with?"

"My dad. Distance riding is his big thing. He's completed the Tevis nine times, and won it twice. I completed it last year."

She pulled up her tee shirt and displayed an ornate belt buckle that said "Tevis" in pearl letters.

Loren went dry-mouthed at the expanse of skin above the belt, but managed to say, "That's great. The Tevis, huh?"

From behind him came a pointed clearing of throat. Loren said, "Oh, um, Sandy, this is my brother Blair Liskey. This is our first ride."

He watched closely as Blair's blindness registered on Sandy. Her face showed a flash of surprise, then a glow of interest.

"Sandy, glad to know you."

She met his outstretched hand, and it seemed to Loren that Blair's handclasp lasted longer than his had. Certainly longer than necessary.

But the three of them were at the table now, and a woman asked their names. "Oh yes," she said, "I have you here. Let's see, I have a notation here. Blair. That's you? You're our blind rider, right? Well, welcome to the Trek, I'm sure you'll get along just fine. You've requested permission to start with your brother. No problem. Here are your rider numbers, fourteen and fifteen to correspond with your stable numbers, and you'll be timed out together when you start. The judges are aware of the situation. Here are your maps of the ride, a list of rules and instructions, and if you have any other questions they'll all be answered tonight at the briefing."

Loren accepted both of their packets. Sandy was a little distance away, whooping and hugging a group of people, apparently old friends.

"Let's go check the horses," he said.

When they arrived at the stable, Kade was moving restlessly in his stall, snatching bites of hay from the swinging net and carrying them to the stall door so that he could watch the alleyway while he chewed. Raven rested within his stall, standing hip-shot and slack-lipped. The boys groomed the travel dust from the horses' hides, then left the animals to rest.

More trailers arrived, unloaded, and pulled away to park among the trees. By midafternoon almost all of the sixty stalls were filled. Tents, pickup campers, vans, and dusty motor homes filled the camping area, and there was steady traffic past the Liskey tent to the restroom building. Everyone spoke or smiled as they passed.

Loren lay on the grass before the tent and studied once again the map of the ride. A similar map had been mailed to him a month ago, when the entries were sent in, so he felt that he already knew the squiggles of red and blue as well as he ever would. The red line was Saturday's trail, and the blue was Sunday's. Each made a loop starting and ending at the rodeo grounds. River crossings were indicated, and dirt roads and bridges, lunch stops and vet checks.

The longer he looked at it, the more tense Loren became. This is it, he thought. All those weeks of working toward it, and here it is. Kade could throw me in front of all these good riders. Or he could spook at a bad place on the trail and kill us both. Or we could come through with flying colors, win the junior trophy, ride off into the sunset with Sandy.

He looked up at Blair, who was chatting with a small child from the neighboring camp.

Am I going to do it to him? Loren wondered. When the time actually comes, am I going to have the guts to do it?

Chapter 8

Blair emerged from the restroom cubicle and paused. To his left was the sound of tap water splashing, and a light scuff of boot on concrete floor.

"Excuse me," he said. "I've got a little vision problem here. I wonder if you could tell me where things are."

"Sure thing." The voice was hearty and adult. Blair was relieved. Kids could be more trouble than they were worth in a situation like this.

The man said, "You got your three, um, stalls, behind you there, and right in front of you are three sinks, and down at the end there, to your right about ten feet, there's a shower stall. Let's see, paper towel holder on the wall in front of you and to the left a little, about shoulder high. What else you need to know?"

"That'll do it," Blair said. "Thanks. I'm Blair Liskey, by the way." He held out his hand and it was accepted by a big hard warm one.

"Dick Watrous, Amarillo. Proud to meet you, Blair. I heard we had a blind rider aboard. Glad you made it. Is this your first ride?"

Blair located the sink, the faucets, the paper towels, while he answered the man's questions. He felt a sense of elation growing within him at this man's acceptance. Watrous, and the others Blair had talked to in the camping area, seemed to view him as a rider, a fellow sportsman enjoying, with them, an exciting activity known to only a small number of people. His blindness was interesting to them primarily as an added challenge on the ride, for which he was to be admired for guts, but nothing more than that. Instead of asking cautious questions about his blindness, these people asked what kind of horse he rode and with what kind of tack, and had he ever tried the Tevis.

"What is the Tevis anyway?" Blair asked. "Somebody was telling me her father won it twice, and I didn't even know what it was."

"Sandy Fields. Ray Fields is probably the top professional distance rider at the Trek, the only Tevis winner, for sure. The Tevis is the granddaddy of distance rides in this country. A hundred miles in a twenty-four-hour period. It's in tough country, right across the Sierras, from Squaw Valley to Auburn, California. It can be a heartbreaker, but anybody who completes it has really accomplished something, and to win it, well, that's as high as you can go in endurance riding, in this country."

Blair left the restroom building thinking about riding one hundred miles in a day, thinking about Sandy Fields. He had a sudden urge to go find her.

"Hey, Loren?" He began making his way in the direction of their tent.

"Lor? Are you there?"

He fell over the lawn chair.

"Hey. Loren. Give me a hand."

But the tent was empty. Blair straightened the lawn chair furiously, and plopped himself into it. That little bastard, he thought. Waited till my back was turned and got away from me. He's with Sandy. Damn. I could never find them in this big an area. I'll just have to sit here till he gets around to coming back. I'd like to punch him out, the little—

But I don't dare. Because tomorrow and the next day I'm going to be at his mercy. Oh, man, am I ever. Up in those mountains with nobody but Loren to keep me on the trail. If ever he wanted a chance to get me, this is it.

"There he is. Blair." A woman's voice called. It was familiar—oh, sure, Blair thought. Alice Boldt, here to cover the ride.

The photographer was with her, and Loren and Sandy Fields. In the instant of greeting, Blair sorted out their voices and assessed the situation. Loren had been with Sandy, scoring points away from Blair, and Miss Boldt had come across him and asked to be taken to Blair, thus breaking up the fun and games with Sandy. Blair heard the resentment in Loren's voice and in his silences.

Sandy seemed cheerfully unaware of fraternal tensions. She chattered with everyone, and went along with the group in high spirits as they moved toward the stable area for pictures of Blair with Raven.

When the pictures were taken and Miss Boldt and Jerry had wandered away in search of interesting people to talk to, Sandy took them to the next row of stalls to see her horse, Margaret. At the stall door Sandy stood delightfully close to Blair and described Margaret.

"She's an Appaloosa-thoroughbred cross, a sort of a red roan with no white feet. That's best for distance riding, because the dark hooves are tougher than the light hooves you get with a stocking. She's about seventeen hands, which is way bigger than a distance horse should be. The better ones are usually the smaller horses, but old Margaret seems to get along better than most big horses. She's fine-boned and lean, with long ears and a kind of Roman nose, not a pretty horse at all, but I love her."

They moved to the next stall. Sandy went on, still close to Blair, "This is my dad's horse, Doc. He's a bay, about fifteen hands. He's a mustang. We got him through that government Adopt-A-Horse program, you know, to find homes for wild horses that were starving. This is Doc's fifth year as a distance horse. My dad can't use him on rides that give cash prizes, because the adoption regulations say you can't use the horses to make money, but my dad likes Doc better than any of his other distance horses. Doc is a real athlete."

They moved along the stable row, peering into stalls, while Sandy greeted people she knew, and explained to Loren and Blair the backgrounds of horses and riders.

"These two black mares over here, they're grandmother and granddaughter, and their riders are a grandmother-granddaughter team, too. Judy is thirteen, this is her second year distance riding. And her grandmother, Mrs. Eubanks, has been doing it even longer than my dad. She's one of my favorite people in the whole world. They live in Oklahoma someplace, and I guess Mom Eubanks is a millionaire, but you'd never know it. She and Judy just spend the whole summer in their pickup camper, going to rides. She loves distance riding. She told me once it was the only thing she'd ever done where her money didn't give her an edge. She's completed the Tevis I don't know how many years, and no amount of money helps you there. People respect her because she's won her Tevis buckle, and I guess that would mean a lot to a rich person who was always getting buttered up for the wrong reasons."

Blair said, "By the way, congratulations yourself, on your Tevis buckle. I didn't get a chance to say anything earlier, but that impresses the heck out of me, a hundred-mile ride in a day, and in country like that."

He heard Loren stop walking, then start again. Hah. Got you there, brother, Blair thought.

Sandy's arm brushed Blair's. She said "Thanks, Blair. I'm kind of proud of that, myself. I don't mind telling you I was a little nervous about that ride. I hadn't had Margaret very long, and I wasn't too sure about her. She's kind of bad about not wanting to be out of sight of the other horses, and that can be a little dangerous on a mountain trail."

"We better start back," Loren said. "The barbecue starts at five, and it's almost that now. And I want to clean up a little bit."

Blair's hand found Sandy's and squeezed. She answered with a quick friendly pressure as they turned to start toward the aroma of steaming beef and barbecue sauce.

Two hours later Blair settled between his parents on a bleacher seat beside the rodeo arena. Loren was on the bench below, with Sandy and her father, Mrs. Eubanks and Judy, all of whom had come together during the barbecue.

Beside him Norma was saying, "—nice gift shops, but I can't say they were really any better than mine, and the prices here are way higher. It was fun going through them, but—"

Blair strained to hear what Loren and Sandy were saying.

The sound system sputtered to life, and the crowd in the bleachers grew still. Blair felt the tension around him.

"Hi there, Trekkies, welcome to the Sangre!"

The woman's voice was answered by spontaneous cheers and greetings from the crowd.

"For those of you who don't already know me, I'm Karen Crow. I think I met most of you as you arrived. First of all, does every rider have a map?"

Blair heard the rustle of maps being waved. I don't have one, he thought. All I've got is Loren.

"Okay, good. If you need a map, see me after the briefing. I think the map is self-explanatory. We start and finish here both days, but the trail will be different each day. The red line is tomorrow's trail, the blue is Sunday's. The trails are well marked with paper plates nailed to trees, red for Saturday's trail and blue for Sunday's. You'll be timed out from right here, in the arena. You'll go straight across the grounds that way, toward that one tall pine that kind of stands alone. Everybody see it?

"Okay. You'll trot your horses from here to the pine, to give the judges a good look at how they're moving. Past the pine, you can go at whatever speed you want. You'll see trail markers starting there. It's an easy wooded trail

102

for about two miles, and coming in each day you'll want to ease upon that stretch, to bring your horses in in the best possible condition. After that two-mile stretch as you're going out, you'll follow a dirt road approximately five miles, then go off to your right on a narrow trail that will take you back into the mountains. You'll cross the lower fork of the Puma River at a ford. The river's three to four feet deep at that point, fairly fast current, and we'll have a team of men there with ropes in case anybody gets in trouble."

Fear washed down through Blair's stomach.

"After that you'll do some climbing, but it's a good trail. You won't have any trouble with it. When you get to the top, there'll be a fifteen-minute vet check, and any horses whose PRs don't come down to a safe level after the fifteen minutes will be asked to drop out.

"You'll be riding a ridge, then, maybe four or five miles, then you'll start a descent. It's a little steep in places, but you shouldn't have any trouble with it. At the bottom you'll cross the upper fork of the Puma. There is a narrow suspension bridge. If you can get your horses onto it, fine. If not, go downstream about fifty, sixty yards and you'll see a place where you can get down into the water to swim them across."

Norma whispered to Blair, "This sounds kind of dangerous, honey. Are you sure you want to do it?"

Blair nodded, grimly.

Karen Crow's voice continued. "After the river you'll have a fairly long uphill climb, but it's not steep. You'll come out into the open at the head of a valley. Go straight across the valley. There won't be trees to put markers on,

103

but you'll be going through a series of gates as you cross privately owned pasture land, and you'll see our men beside each gate.

"At the far end of the valley is our lunch stop—hooray—in the town of Eagle's Watch. Lunch will be served by the citizens of Eagle's Watch. All twelve of them."

Laughter.

"The stop is a mandatory one hour. You'll be timed in and timed out again at the end of your individual hour. Horses will be checked very thoroughly, of course, and those that aren't in passable shape will be eliminated."

Oh yes please, Blair thought.

The voice went on, brightly. "After lunch you'll leave town going north along the road for about a mile, then turn right, and you're back in the hills again. It's a beautiful trail. I think you're all going to enjoy the scenery, if you've got enough strength left to look at it. The afternoon trail will bring you around in a big loop back toward Majestad. You'll be at the highest elevation of the whole ride, so those of you whose horses aren't accustomed to it, watch them. We don't want any casualties. Now, there will be some pretty narrow stretches in that afternoon segment, and I want to remind you all, and especially you juniors, not to try to pass a strange horse where the trail is narrow. You never know when a horse might spook or rear or kick at a passing horse, and it can be dangerous. Seriously. There are a few of us old folks who get kind of bad about that, too, but you kids tend to get carried away with the racing sometimes, so remember.

"You'll cross the Puma River again, but this time you'll be crossing it above the fork, so you'll only cross once. There is a bridge, not very wide and it doesn't have side rails, but you should be able to get across it okay. I would not advise trying to swim the river at that point, because it is deep and fast, and you're just upstream from some pretty good-sized falls. The current could carry you over, so don't try it."

"Neal," Norma whispered, "I don't know—"

"From the river on, it's an easy ride. Another fifteen-minute vet check, and after that you'll be on jeep trails most of the way. You'll come out of the timber on this same dirt road you went out on, then the two miles of easy trail, come out by the big pine, across the rodeo grounds, and into the arena."

A few voices cheered the end of the imaginary ride.

The woman's voice went on. "I won't brief you on Sunday's trail till tomorrow night. Those of you who are still with us then." Low laughter.

"After ten o'clock tonight, no one but the stable crew will be allowed in the stable area, so please don't try. Get your horses taken care of before then, because there will be no exceptions to the rule. From ten tonight until four forty-five tomorrow morning, you will not be allowed in the stable area. You'll have from four forty-five till six to get your horses fed, watered, groomed, and tacked up.

"Preliminary checks start at six here in the arena, and there will be coffee, hot chocolate, fruit, and rolls available for the riders, in the arena, from six to eight while the prelims are being done.

"First riders will leave at eight sharp, and every thirty seconds thereafter. We'll start with the heavyweight division riders, then lightweight, then novice, then juniors. We've got, let's see, eleven heavyweight, eighteen lightweight, twenty-one novice, and fourteen junior riders; however, some won't pass the prelims, so be alert for your turn to leave. You'll go in numerical order within your division.

"Well, that covers my end of things. Now I'd like to introduce our judges, who will each say a few words. First, our veterinary judge, Doctor Alan Ruden, from Redondo Beach, California. Doctor Ruden?"

A man's voice, full of youthful enthusiasm began, as the applause died. "Thanks for the applause, but it won't help you a bit if your PRs are off."

Laughter rose around Blair.

"I'll be brief, here. I know you all want to get lots of rest tonight. You've got a big day ahead of you. You all know what I'll be checking for tomorrow: temperatures, pulse and respiration beyond normal ranges, sore backs, saddle sores or tack abrasions of any kind, cracked hooves, foot problems or leg problems that could be worsened by a fifty-mile ride. I'll be checking for inversions, that is, a respiration count going higher than the pulse. If they're both reasonably low I won't be concerned, but if you're coming in with a horse with an eighty-five pulse and a ninety-five respiration rate, you're going to be out of the game. If I see serious interference marks on your horse's pasterns, same thing.

"I want you all to know that I hope every single one of you completes the ride. Nothing would make me happier. But one of my primary functions here this weekend is to make sure no horse is pushed beyond his safe limit of exertion, and to head off injuries to horse and rider as best I can. Hopefully none of you wants to win so badly that you'd endanger your horse's well-being, and I'm here to see that you don't. I've officiated at a number of distance

106

rides now, and I'm always impressed with the sportsman-
ship that you people show, and with your concern for your
animals. Good luck to each and every one of you."

Through the slowly dying applause came Karen Crow's
voice again. "Thank you, Alan. Now I'd like to introduce
our lay judge, Mrs. Maralee Kramar, of Huntingburg,
Ohio. Mrs. Kramar is one of the country's leading author-
ities on distance riding, and a two-time Tevis winner.
Mrs. Kramar."

Her speech was short and to the point, listing some of
the things she would be watching for, and wishing each
rider a safe and successful Trek.

When it was over Karen Crow asked for questions.
There was silence. Then Blair heard Loren's voice.

"What if someone gets lost?"

His voice held a note of tension, almost excitement, carefully concealed from any ears but Blair's supersensitive
ones. Again, fear washed over Blair.

Karen Crow answered. "There will be a pair of drag
riders following the last riders. No, not wearing dresses,"
she said humorously, in response to what must have been
a standing joke. "They'll be on the lookout for any strays,
but really, it shouldn't be a problem. The trail markers are
easy to see. I don't think you could get lost if you tried.
And all riders will be accounted for at the check stops, of
course. If anyone is overly late getting in, someone will
come looking for them. Also, I should mention, we'll have
a trailer stationed at each break, so if your horse is injured
we can get him trailered out for you. Any other questions?"

There were none. The people around Blair began
stretching, shifting, standing to descend the bleachers.

Norma said, "Neal, I don't know about all this. From what that first speaker said, it sounds like it's going to be pretty dangerous out there tomorrow, especially for Blair. What do you think?"

Before Neal could answer, Blair heard Sandy's voice, low and in front of him. "You don't need to worry, Mrs. Liskey. I've done this ride three years now and it sounds much worse than it really is. And besides, there used to be a blind guy out in Utah that did these rides for years. He never had any trouble, and I know Blair won't either."

Blair could hear the smile in her voice. He wanted to hug her, to touch her at least. But Loren was there.

Neal said, "Honey, the boys will be fine. Blair's got Loren to look after him. So quit making mother-noises, and let's get back to our motel and let these young folks enjoy themselves. We'll see you guys about seven o'clock, okay?"

"Night, you two." Blair grinned toward his parents and successfully hid a near-panic feeling of being cut adrift from his moorings.

Blair, Loren, Sandy, and her father wandered back to the stable for a final check on the horses, then went to the Fields' pickup camper where they were soon joined by the Eubanks, grandmother and granddaughter, and several other riders who were apparently old friends of the Fields'.

Blair sat on the ground with his back against the wheel of the horse trailer and thought how good this moment would be if he didn't have to think about tomorrow. The talk drifted around him, laughing reminiscences of past rides, comparisons of new composition horseshoes and Maclellan versus endurance saddles.

Blair concentrated on Sandy's position. First it was near her father. Then it shifted to the right, where Loren was. Then, miraculously, she settled close beside him and her hand found his in the darkness.

After a while Blair whispered, "Could you walk me over to the restroom building? I hate to take Loren away from the fun."

"Sure."

When he judged that they were near his tent he said, "I have a better idea. Let's step into my parlor. Just for a minute."

She hesitated. "I thought you were wanting the restroom."

"I lied." He grinned. "Come on, we'll just sit and talk, just for a little while, okay? I haven't had a chance to get to know you, and I really do want to."

"Well—"

They went into the tent and sat side by side, cross-legged, on Blair's air mattress bed. "Listen, Sandy, please don't take this the wrong way, but I really would like to see you, and the only way I can do that is—braille. Would you mind? I don't have any idea what you look like."

"Well, okay, but watch it."

Softly he traced the lines of her face with his fingertips; her eyebrows, the curve of her nose and lips. The lips were warm, and he felt a throb in them. Her lashes brushed his skin as her eyes closed.

He kissed her.

His senses went dizzy, but a clear, cold corner of his mind said, Score one against you, Loren.

His braille exploration continued, down her throat, over the ridge of her collarbone—

"Well, excuse me all to pieces," Loren said from the door. "I didn't realize this tent was such a busy place."

Sandy jerked away and scrambled to her feet. "I've got to get back, anyway. Four o'clock comes early. See you Blair, Loren."

And she was gone.

Wordlessly Blair and Loren stripped to their underwear and crawled into their sleeping bags.

Blair said, "Did you set the alarm clock?"

"Yes. What were you trying with her, anyway, Blair? You knew I liked her."

"So? I like her, too. All's fair in love—"

"And distance riding, hermano. And you're going to get yours." Loren's voice dropped to a whisper.

Long after Loren was asleep, Blair lay rigid with fear in his down-filled cocoon.

I wasn't imagining it, he thought. Loren is out to get me.

And tomorrow, the trail . . .

Chapter 9

The alarm ripped through the tent at four-thirty. Loren silenced it, then lay relishing the warmth and safety of his sleeping bag. Out there in the dark, Kade was waiting. Kade and fifty miles of mountain trail.

Blair was already crouched over their suitcase, shivering and groping. Loren joined him. Cold damp night air filled the tent. It was almost more than Loren could do to strip to his goosebump skin and pull on the silk-and-cotton long underwear that his distance-riding book had suggested to prevent chafing. Over the underwear went soft old jeans, soft enough not to rub at the seams, a loose-weave cotton shirt for the hot part of the day, wool sweater, and rainproof poplin jacket. Soft, bulky socks protected his feet and legs from any possible boot-rubbing.

Blair snapped open his watch and touched the face. "It's quarter of five already. I thought you were going to set the alarm for four."

"I changed my mind. Figured four-thirty would give us plenty of time, and it did. All we have to do is run over to the bathroom, and if we'd got up earlier we'd have had to stand in line to get in there. Besides, we're going to have plenty of time to stand around and get nervous before eight o'clock. You ready? Let's go."

By the time they'd finished in the rest-room building and reached the stable, the sky was a pale apple green behind the mountains. Ground mist wafted among the trees and obliterated the far end of the stable buildings. Loren was fully awake now. There was a sense of unreality about the dawn and the place that made him wish he could relax and enjoy it.

Neal and Norma appeared, shivering and yawning, and together the four of them went to the stalls.

Kade was pacing, stirring the straw with his nervous movements.

"He looks like he hasn't slept all night," Loren said grimly. "He's going to burn himself out before we even get started."

Raven greeted them with a stretch and a mammoth yawn. I wish Kade would relax more, Loren thought.

Then there was no more time for thinking. There was grain to be measured carefully and served; hay to be stuffed into the swinging hay bays, one flake for each horse; water to be carried from the hydrant down the row.

Norma said, "Don't worry about cleaning the stalls, honey. Dad and I can do that after you've gone. We're going to have time to kill before we head up to the lunch stop."

"Can you find your way up there all right?" Loren asked.

"No problem. We met some other people last night at the motel that'll be driving up, too. We'll go with them."

When the horses finished their grain and were working their way more slowly through their hay, Loren and Blair began grooming. They curried and brushed and toweled until every speck of dust, every loose hair, was gone. Each hoof was picked up and gouged clean with the hoof pick, then checked with fingertips for any buried bit of rock, anything that might be hidden under the rim of the shoe or in the deep V-shaped valley beside the frog. Every horseshoe nail was checked to be sure it was tight.

All along the rows of stalls, similar preparations were underway for every horse. In one stall a sorrel gelding was found to have a slight leg injury, probably from the trailer trip. He had come fourteen hundred miles, from Atlanta, Georgia. His young owner fought back tears of disappointment as she went to notify the judges of her withdrawal.

"It's almost six," Neal called. He and Norma handed into the stalls two freshly laundered, fleecy white saddle pads, two saddles gleaming with elbow grease, two bridles carefully cleaned and checked for rough places that might rub sores on a sweating horse's head.

As the first direct rays of morning sun came over the trees to chase away the fog, Loren and Blair emerged, leading El Kadir and Raven. The chestnut was full of himself, arching his neck and tail and moving sideways against the restrictive hold on his bridle. Raven came placidly, still mouthing the last of his hay.

A river of horses flowed toward the arena, some led, some ridden. Each rider wore a square of cloth across his chest and back, tied in place with narrow strips and bearing his rider number.

Loren said, "Mom, I forgot our numbers. Would you get them? They're in the tent, and would you get our knee bandages, too?"

The arena seemed filled with milling horses and darting children. Men and women bearing clipboards and stopwatches were everywhere.

One woman, spotting Loren, said, "Juniors over this way, please. You guys don't need to be weighed, so we'll get through you a little faster. If you'll just stay in this area till you've been checked—" and she was gone.

Loren leaned against Kade's saddle and tried to look calm. His hands trembled. He felt his jacket pocket for the map. It was there. Norma appeared, and harnessed him into his number fourteen bib while Neal did Blair's. Then Norma wrapped each boy's knees in the elastic bandages that would ease the strain of standing in stirrups all day.

Sandy appeared, leading Margaret. She waved and gave Loren a stiff smile, but made no effort to come close. Loren couldn't tell whether she was embarrassed about last night, or nervous about the ride. Her appearance reminded him of last night's anger at Blair, but for now he was too tense about the coming ride to want to think about Sandy. Time for that later.

Alice Boldt and Jerry arrived and Blair posed, smiling, for pictures. He pretended to check Raven's cinch, his hoof, his bridle. Loren looked away.

Teenagers began circulating among the waiting riders with trays of coffee, cocoa, and juice, and huge cardboard boxes of rolls and doughnuts. Loren took an orange juice and a glazed doughnut, but had to struggle to get them down.

After an incredibly long wait, the team of judges finally approached.

"Fourteen," Dr. Ruden said, consulting his clipboard.

114

"El Kadir, am I pronouncing that right? Half-Arab gelding, six years old, Loren Liskey? Well, let's check him out."

Kade shied away from the cold touch of the thermometer under his tail, but Dr. Ruden was firm and agile.

"Nice-looking animal," Dr. Ruden said, smiling. "This your first ride?"

Loren nodded. "Does it show?"

The man's smile warmed. "You do look a little pale around the gills, but then so do lots of the veteran riders. You just relax and have a good time, and you'll be fine. Looks like good weather, and you'll be riding through some of the most beautiful scenery in the country."

Kade relaxed as the thermometer came out. The doctor wiped it clean, read it, made a notation on his chart. Then he wriggled his stethoscope into place and pressed it against Kade's ribs, just behind his elbow. The stopwatch clicked, and clicked again, and another figure was noted. Then the man placed his hand lightly over Kade's flanks and studied the watch again, counting the rise and fall of Kade's breathing.

While this was going on, the other judge, the woman from Ohio, strolled around Kade, studying him through slitted eyes.

Dr. Ruden said to her, "Temp one-oh-one point one, pulse fifty-eight, respiration forty-four. A shade high, but he's a little excited."

At Dr. Ruden's request Loren unsaddled Kade, then stood back while the doctor went over every inch of the horse's hide, checking for old or new scars, saddle sores, marks of any kind. He stood and said to the other judge, as he wrote on his chart, "Very slight old interference

115

mark, inside pastern on left fore, just above coronet. Otherwise, clean as a newborn calf."

Mrs. Kramar, the lay judge, asked Loren to lead Kade away from her in a straight line at a trot, then straight back. Loren tried, but Kade was full of bedsprings. Time and again he danced sideways, snorting at the other horses and fighting to go faster.

"That's good enough," the woman called finally.

The team of judges moved on to Blair, and Loren heard Dr. Ruden say, "Oh yes, you're our blind rider. Well, welcome aboard, and good luck. I'm sure you'll get along just fine."

As Loren resaddled and pulled Kade's front legs forward one at a time, to smooth any wrinkled skin that might be pinched in the girth, he watched the judging team go over Raven.

"Temp one-oh-one even. Pulse, forty. Respiration, forty."

Loren held his breath.

The judging team went on to examine Raven's body for marks and to watch his movement for signs of unsoundness. Norma led the horse, who moved sluggishly and wouldn't trot until Neal slapped his rump.

"That's fine," Mrs. Kramar called. To Blair she said, "Now, you'll be riding with your brother, number fourteen, is that right? Fine, then, I'm sure you won't have any trouble. Good luck."

Loren turned away to recheck the tightness of his cinch. So. We both made it through the vet check. Now there's nothing to stop Blair . . . but me. And nothing to stop me except him.

And then, too soon, it was eight o'clock and the first

riders were being released, one at a time at thirty-second intervals, and the ride began.

Kade danced under Loren in reaction to the excitement around him and the tension he felt in Loren's legs and hands.

Karen Crow called, "Novices next. Get yourselves lined up in numerical order, so we can tick you right off as you go. Number sixteen—go! Seventeen—go! Eighteen—go!"

Now the judges were positioned just beyond the arena entrance, where they would watch the horses trotting across the open expanse of grass toward the pine tree. One of the novice horses showed a limp and was pulled out. The others went on in a steady rhythm like drops from a faucet, at precise thirty-second intervals.

"Juniors, get ready, you're next," Karen Crow called.

Thirteen riders, all in their teens, glanced at one another's numbers and positioned their horses accordingly. Loren and Blair were last.

An elderly woman, one of the clipboard crew, said to Loren, "We can't release you boys at exactly the same time because the judges need to get a clear view of each horse's movement as you start. But we cut the interval to fifteen seconds, and you'll be going first. We figured your brother's horse would still follow okay, at that distance, and you can wait for him to catch up when you get to the tree. Will that work out all right for you both?"

Loren nodded. His mouth was too dry for words. Blair said, "Sure. No problem."

His voice sounded normal. And he's going into it blind, Loren thought. Here I am about to throw up, and he's not turning a hair.

Kade half-reared, and fought for his head.

The rider ahead of Loren was sent off.

"Number fourteen—go."

Kade leaped forward, half-cantering, wanting to get his head down so he could buck. Loren jerked more savagely than he meant to. Kade propped and did a sideways jump, then shook his head and settled into a trot, his eyes on the horse ahead of him just disappearing into the wooded trail.

Behind him, Loren heard Karen Crow's voice calling jubilantly, "Number fifteen—go! That's it, troops. They're on their way."

Now that the waiting was over, Loren felt slightly better. Blair and Raven were close behind as they passed the pine tree with its red-and-blue paper plates nailed on, and entered the cool green tunnel of the jeep trail.

They moved at a brisk trot. Loren was aware of the fifty-some horses strung out ahead of him, out of sight already, and he felt a sense of being the last runner in a race. He knew that the winner would be the horse who finished the two days with the shortest actual riding time and in good physical condition, not just the first horse in on Sunday night. But the feeling persisted.

If I can get Blair off my back, he thought, so I don't have to hold back to his speed, then I'd have a fair shot at it. Otherwise, all I'm here for is to lead him to fame and glory. Nuts to that.

By the time they emerged from the jeep trail to the dirt road, Kade's trot was so extended that Loren had to stand in his stirrups to ease the jolt of his body on Kade's backbone. He glanced back. Blair was following with apparent nonchalance, a bland smile on his face. He, too, was standing to avoid the jolt of Raven's rough trot. Behind Blair, the two drag riders emerged from the trees wearing broad pale chaps and tall-crowned hats.

Although the road was little more than a dirt track and obviously not accustomed to traffic, it was lined this morning with cars, pickups, bicycles, and local people who grinned and waved to the riders, and called "Good luck," as Loren and Blair passed.

"Here comes Blair Liskey," a childish voice called. "Yay Blair. Go get 'em."

Blair waved toward the voice and grinned. Loren thought, The word must be out, about Blair. Hell, they're going to make a hero out of him. Well, we'll see about that.

To give their standing muscles a rest and to take advantage of the level roadway, Loren put Kade into a canter, and Raven followed. Kade made no attempt to buck. Loren relaxed a bit more, and looked around.

The road led through a stand of Douglas fir and blue spruce. The deep blue-green of the forest had a quality of liquid light to it almost like that of ocean water. Thin, clear air intensified the ribbon of sunlight that followed the road. The air was cool against Loren's face.

A red paper plate appeared on a tree at Loren's right. He slowed to a walk, against Kade's wishes.

At first the trail was as broad and easy as the jeep trail had been, a double track covered with pine needles and churned by the hooves of the horses ahead. But soon it narrowed and began to climb. It followed the side of the slope, and although the trail was no wider than a horse, the upward slope on the right and the downward slope on the left were shallow enough to reassure Loren. Even if Kade spooked here, nothing too bad would happen.

But after the first switchback the trail grew noticeably steeper. The horses slowed to a moderate trot, and in places where the trail was badly churned by the other horses, Kade had to scramble for his footing.

One more switchback, and the trees on the downhill side opened to reveal a panorama of valleys and peaks, gray-green and blue-green up close, fading to silver and mauve in the distance.

But Loren didn't see it. He was straining now with Kade's every movement and trying not to think of the dropoff beside him.

Abruptly the trail leveled, then began to descend. "Going down," Loren called to Blair.

The descent seemed longer than the climb, but less frightening. Trees welcomed them down into the valley, and blocked out distant views. Loren could hear the drag riders above him, talking easily and laughing. Stripes of sun and shade crossed him as the trees thickened.

He heard water rushing, then saw the sparkle of a small river below. Two men on horseback, with coiled ropes on their saddles, waited beside the ford. One had a clipboard.

"Fourteen and fifteen," he said as Loren rode up. "That's everybody safe and accounted for." He grinned and waved Loren toward the ford.

Kade waded in willingly, but Raven had other ideas. He touched the water with one front hoof, and spun away from it. One of the drag riders came up beside Blair and popped Raven with his quirt. Raven leaped into the water, but Blair was ready for the leap this time, and stayed aboard.

The bed of the stream was covered with mossy rocks. Kade slipped and stumbled slightly, caught himself, and picked his way across with greater caution after that. Icy water rose above Loren's boot tops, soaking his jeans and trickling down into his socks.

For a few yards in midstream the horses swam. Then they were in the shallows again, and plunging up onto the bank.

"Okay?" Loren called over his shoulder.

"Okay. A little damp is all," Blair answered.

Abruptly the trail began to climb. Here there were areas of bare shale rock, over which the horses had to scramble for their footing. Loren's heart stopped as Kade slipped, went to his knees, came up again.

At a switchback the grade became so steep that Loren halted Kade and said, "I'm going to get off and tail him up this next stretch."

He dismounted, and almost fell as his tension-numbed legs folded under him. Blair dismounted, too. Loren looped his reins around the saddle horn with plenty of slack so Kade could throw his head forward, attached his long rope, then moved back to grasp Kade's tail, and called, "Gee-up."

Kade lunged, and Loren scrambled, stumbled, pulled himself up by Kade's tail. At the top Kade halted on his own, and Loren had to move him forward to make room for Raven, who had followed closely behind. Loren noticed that Kade's legs were trembling, and sweat dripped from the horse's belly. Kade's sides pumped in and out as he fought for breath. Raven seemed tired, too, but calmer than Kade.

The trail rose at a somewhat more benign angle after that, and horses began to appear on the path ahead. The trees opened, and the riders emerged on a small barren plateau filled with milling horses, stiff-legged, dismounted riders, and the clipboard brigade.

As Loren dismounted a woman appeared at Kade's head, already writing on her clipboard. "Number fourteen, time in, ten-thirty-three." Loren stretched and watched as the woman counted Kade's pulse and respiration, and jotted down her figures. A man, the white-haired man who had greeted them yesterday at the stable, was checking Raven.

The woman said to Loren, "Ninety-six over ninety-two. That's a little high. If I were you I'd walk him the whole fifteen minutes, over away from the other horses, to try to get those counts down."

Loren nodded but stayed near Blair and Raven while the old man applied a stethoscope to Raven's ribs and stared at his stopwatch. "Sixty, pulse."

Blair's face was impassive. Loren studied it, trying to understand Blair's calm. Did he want to go on? Was he hoping to be vetted out?

The man cupped his hand over Raven's nostril, clicked his watch, clicked again. "Sixty-eight," he said, frowning. "Dr. Ruden, we've got an inversion here, want to check?"

Loren pulled in his breath and held it. If Raven is vetted out now, he thought, I'll be free of them, and I won't have to use Plan B. Oh, please!

Dr. Ruden checked the figures and swept Raven with an intent stare. "We'll wait and see how he checks out at the end of the fifteen minutes."

Both Loren and Blair relaxed somewhat, but it would have been difficult for anyone, even the boys, to know whether the relaxation was relief or disappointment.

As Loren plodded in his solitary circle with an unusually

subdued Kade at his shoulder, he wondered if he himself wanted to be eliminated. He wondered if there were rougher, steeper parts of the trail yet to come, or if this was as bad as it was going to get.

A PR checker with nothing more to do came and offered to walk Kade. Gratefully Loren handed him over and stretched out on the ground for three or four blissful minutes.

Then the fifteen minutes were up, and Kade's PR readings were retaken. "Sixty, and forty-four," the woman said to Dr. Ruden, who added them to his chart and compared them with the previous figures.

"Coming down in pretty good shape," he said to Loren. "You can go on."

Dr. Ruden and Mrs. Kramar approached Raven, who by now was cropping grass in the shade. While one counted his pulsebeats, the other counted breaths. Loren mounted Kade and rode close.

"Pulse, thirty-six."

"Got thirty-two here. Okay, you can go on."

Plan B began to look like a probable necessity.

Four horses stood at the side of the clearing. They had failed the check and would be ridden back to Majestad at a careful pace, then trailered home by their disappointed riders.

The timer waved at Loren to start and noted his starting time. Loren guided Kade past the first paper-plated tree, then slowed for Raven to catch up. The trail followed a high ridge whose only trees were low-growing junipers. On either side the land sloped away in rolling vistas magnified by the thin air and bright sunlight. Loren shrugged out of his jacket and tied its arms around his waist. Other

123

riders were in view not far ahead, going singly or in groups of two or three and most moving at a ground-covering trot.

Loren let Kade increase his speed, and Raven followed. They drew even with the rider ahead and passed her. Before they left the open ease of the ridge, they had passed three more riders. Sandy, on her roan mare, was just two riders ahead of Loren. He wanted to catch up, but Raven was lagging now, and Blair called for Loren to slow down.

Abruptly the trail tightened and dropped, and for the next twenty minutes Loren forgot about Blair and Raven and everything except guiding Kade to the best possible footing and keeping his own weight balanced as well as he could as Kade's head and neck disappeared from sight and no force but sheer will kept Loren from toppling forward.

Twice he jumped off and led Kade down an especially treacherous stretch, on the theory that it would be better to have Kade step on him than for them both to go somersaulting into space. Blair elected to stay in the saddle.

Gradually the angle of descent lessened, and once again a river appeared below. This time there was a narrow footbridge across it that moved slightly in the breeze. None of the horses ahead of Loren would go onto the bridge, and Loren bypassed it without a try.

This ford was somewhat rougher and deeper than the first, but Raven went in without serious hesitation. The cold water was less unpleasant against Loren's legs than it had been earlier.

The next climb was no worse than the first one earlier that morning, and by now Loren was beginning to grow accustomed to the scrambling and the sudden dropoffs that appeared without warning, just beyond Kade's shoulder. He kept his attention riveted to the trail ahead.

At last the open valley Karen Crow had described was unfolding itself before Loren. It was a sight more beautiful than any he'd ever seen. Just an easy ride down some sloping meadowland, and there, in the distance, Eagle's Watch, and lunch.

Chapter 10

The riders descended the valley at a trot, and the men at each gate waved them through, grinning. The line of horses emerged from the long meadow grass just at the edge of the town.

"I don't believe this place," Loren said to Blair as they trotted up the dusty street. "It's right off Warner Brothers' back lot. One dirt road up the middle of town, old wooden buildings, wooden sidewalks even. All it needs is John Wayne and a few injuns."

Blair chuckled, and for an instant Loren felt an old warmth left over from childhood, the fun of describing things to Blair so he could share Loren's enjoyment of them.

Again the horses' individual arrival times were noted, and PRs taken. Neal and Norma appeared and relieved the boys of their horses, who had to be walked and cooled. With Blair's hand on his shoulder Loren followed the arrows to the restrooms, in a saloon that matched the town's movie-set atmosphere.

The two emerged again into the sun and got paper plates loaded with sloppy joes and baked beans and potato salad. They collapsed, along with other riders, on the wooden sidewalk, their backs against the buildings, their feet protruding from the shade.

Norma and Neal appeared, still leading the horses. "Loosen their cinches and kind of lift the saddles a time or two," Loren called. "Give them a little water, but not too much till they finish cooling off. I think you could quit walking them now."

Loren made a pillow of his jacket and sweater, and slid down until he was lying flat across the sidewalk. His body still thrummed with the motion of the horse and his legs ached, his back ached, his head ached.

I'll never make it, he thought.

To Blair he said, "How you feeling?"

"Great. No problem."

"Me too," Loren chirped. He flexed his legs and tried to smooth a wrinkle that had formed in his jeans, inside one of his knee bandages. It had already chafed a raw place just where his knees gripped the saddle. He felt exhausted beyond anything he'd felt on a training ride even though only twenty-six miles were done. Nervous tension, he told himself. The vision of the junior division trophy receded from his mind. All he could think of now was getting through the next few hours.

Time to get up. Time to resaddle and report to the PR crew for the checkout. "Let's go, Blair." He kicked his brother's foot.

Kade's checkout readings were well within normal limits. Raven's were even better.

Once again, Loren sighed and mounted.

After lunch the trail rose again, in some places so steeply and narrowly that Loren could only focus his eyes on Kade's mane and pray. No longer was he worried about the horse shying or bucking. All of El Kadir's energy went into getting up the next climb. The horse trembled with exhaustion but went on, on nervous energy alone. Raven followed stolidly.

Up, over the crest, and down again to another river-threaded valley floor. As they approached the bridge, Loren's tension mounted. This was it. The worst part of the day. The narrow plank bridge stretched across the river, no wider than car tracks, and without side rails.

There were no other riders close to Loren and Blair, either in front or behind. No one to give Kade a lead across.

"Well, here goes nothing." He aimed Kade at the bridge. The horse put one foot on it, looked over the edge at the swirling water below, and spun away, his courage for once deserting him. Loren dismounted and tried to lead him across.

No, Kade said firmly with flattened ears and planted feet.

"Want me to try?" Blair said.

"You want to?"

"No, not really, but unless you have some better idea—"

"Okay, we'll try it. Come forward about ten feet, and just to the left, no, not that far, more to the—there, straight ahead, now you got it."

Raven lowered his head to examine the bridge, but stepped onto it after just a slight pause. Quickly Loren maneuvered behind him and led Kade ahead. With a familiar horse to follow, Kade stepped onto the bridge and clopped across.

"Whew," Loren said as he remounted. "Thanks, brother. I didn't think we were going to survive that one."

"Can't keep two good men down."

They laughed and rode on.

Again the trail climbed, but this time it was comfortably pitched and Loren could relax and look around.

"This is some place," he called back over his shoulder. "The rocks are layered, white rock and sort of goldish, and reddish brown. And over on the left it's all huge pine trees with little clearings here and there, like a park, and I can see some deer way down there. Or they might be moose, no, deer. And from up here you can just see range after range of mountains. I never knew the Sangres were this big. This is more like the Rockies."

The climb ended with another fifteen-minute vet check. Both horses passed, but several others had been eliminated during the day. The PR girl who checked Raven told them that only nine of the fourteen junior division riders were still in the game.

"Let's push for some speed on this last part," Loren said as they left the checkpoint. "If the other riders are dropping like flies, we might have a shot at placing in this insane race."

They were on a jeep road that followed a narrow valley. It was relatively smooth and level, an ideal place to make time. Kade was willing to stretch into a fast trot, but Raven hung back. He was near the end of his strength, and he wouldn't be pushed.

One by one the other junior riders eased past them. When at last Kade and Raven trotted across the rodeo grounds and into the arena, no one was behind them but the drag riders.

Loren clenched his jaw and fought down his disappointment. He hated having Kade bested by the other horses when he could feel Kade's unspent eagerness. The mellow-ness he'd felt toward Blair that afternoon, a sense of team-work at the bridge and the pleasure of trying to share his sight with his brother, faded under the pressure of time and competition passing.

As they entered the arena they were met by the inevita-ble clipboards and stopwatches. When Loren's PR girl began her check of Kade's pulse, Loren swung to the ground. His legs, numbed to uselessness, collapsed and let him fall to the ground.

Flushing, he scrambled up and stood gripping his stirrup for support. "Never did that before," he muttered. From the corner of his lowered gaze he saw Alice Boldt and her photographer recording the moment.

The PR girl stopped counting, jotted down a figure, and said, "Don't worry about it, it happens all the time at the end of the first day. Your legs are under a lot more strain than you think they are on a ride as steep as this one. You can take your horse back to the stable now and take care of him. The stable area will be closed after eight o'clock, and the judges will examine all the horses after that, in the stable. You won't be needed. They're serving supper over there when you're ready."

Neal and Norma appeared with grins and hugs and pride, and led the way back to stalls fourteen and fifteen.

"What can we do to help?" Norma asked.

Loren tried to remember what the book had said to do at the end of the day. Loosen the cinch but don't take the saddle off for several minutes or you'll get heat bumps. A little hay and a very little water, a third of a bucket every fifteen minutes for the first hour, or was it a fourth of a bucket every thirty minutes? His brain was groggy with the strain of the day, and his muscles ached beyond belief. His legs and rear were losing their numbness now, and he regretted the loss.

"Loren?" Norma said, jogging his elbow.

"Oh, yeah. I don't know. Um, I think the riders are supposed to do their own horses. Maybe you could bring us some supper and we could eat while we work."

He and Kade stumbled into their stall while Blair felt his way into Raven's. Blair said, "How you doing?"

"Okay. You?"

"Sore as a boil, but otherwise okay. I wonder how Sandy did."

"Don't know. I didn't see her after lunch. She was probably way out ahead of us. We can take off their bridles and loosen cinches. Can you find his halter in there? Is he hot under his chest?"

"Not really," Blair said. "Got a lot of dried sweat but he feels pretty cool. Uh, yeah, got his halter."

For nearly an hour they worked over the horses, offering hay, grain, and water in cautious amounts, sponging away sweat and crusted trail dirt, and spending long, weary, aching moments squeezing and rubbing the horses' muscles. From time to time Loren paused to lean against Kade and eat a few bites of the cold chicken supper Norma held for him.

His mother and father sat on upturned buckets just outside the stall doors, chattering about their day and the people they'd met, but Loren didn't hear the words. He was tuned into Kade. As he worked each muscle in the horse's body beneath his finger and palms, he could feel the exact moment when the tension left it and the muscle grew relaxed and comfortable. It fascinated him. With his

131

own muscles crying for ease, Loren imagined the relief he was giving his horse, and the gratitude that Kade was probably feeling. Love glowed in Loren. Kade wasn't the enemy now, to be feared and battled and conquered—he was the partner whose courage and spirit had carried Loren through a grueling day. And now the handsome brown animal was leaning into the hands that pressed the tension from the crest of his neck.

So intrigued was Loren by the strength of his feeling for Kade that he barely noticed the rest of the family starting back toward the tent. But when they were gone he realized that his massaging was done, and Kade needed only rest now. He left the stall and went across the stable area to see if Margaret was in her stall.

The mare was there, and so was the girl, with tear streaks on her filthy face.

"Sandy, what's the matter?" Loren was in the stall and reaching for the girl in one instinctive movement.

She turned and buried her head in his shoulder, although she had to bend down a little to do it.

"Margaret got vetted out at the noon check. She had the thumps. I don't know why I'm crying now. I didn't, all afternoon. I just came in to tell her goodnight before they close the stable area, and she just looked so—like she was apologizing for letting me down, or something."

"Aw, darn," Loren murmured into her hair. He ached for Sandy's disappointment, but blessed Margaret and her thumps, whatever they were, for this moment of closeness.

A few minutes later the stable boss came down the row calling, "Eight o'clock, lock-up time. Everybody out."

Loren and Sandy emerged, and the man said to them,

"The briefing session starts in ten minutes at the bleachers. Better get over there."

They went by the tent for Blair, but were headed off by Neal and Norma, who were just getting into their car. "He's asleep," Norma said. "He was just exhausted. Why don't you leave him, Lorey? You can get the briefing information and fill him in. Don't stay up late now. See you in the morning."

The briefing session was a short one. Karen Crow gave a quick rundown on tomorrow's trail, and announced that, of the sixty-four riders who started, forty-one were still in the running.

"And there will probably be some horses who won't pass the final check tonight," she said. "Those figures are about par for the course. Today's ride will have eliminated most of the horses who just weren't fit enough. We'll lose a few more tomorrow, but not as many as today. Well, folks, I know you're tired, so I won't keep you. Checks start at six in the morning, and we'll start timing out at eight again. See you then."

There was a party going on at Ray Fields' camper when Loren walked Sandy home, but neither he nor Sandy felt up to it, so she walked him home instead, and they sat in the lawn chairs outside the tent.

Loren reached for her hand. After a second she withdrew it.

"What's the matter? Is it my breath?" he teased. "Is my deodorant letting me down, or aren't my teeth white enough for sex appeal?"

She looked uncomfortable in the darkness. "It's not you. It's—"

She made a little motion with her head toward the tent behind them.

"Blair?" Loren's voice broke, crackling up an octave.

She nodded.

"What about Blair. He's asleep, he won't hear us."

"No. That's not it. I just feel sort of, you know."

"No, I don't know. You feel what?"

"Fickle. I mean last night I was with him, and here I am tonight—"

"Well, so what? What difference does that make?" Tension and anger began to grow in Loren.

"It makes a lot of difference to me," she retorted. "I really like Blair. I think he's one gutsy guy to do what he's doing. I don't think I could. You've got to admire a man who goes after things the way he does. He doesn't let his blindness stop him one bit. I've never met anyone like him in my life."

"That's just because he's blind," Loren shot back. "If I was the one that was blind, you'd like me better, right? Is that what it takes?"

"No, of course not. That's not it. It's just, I don't know—"

She subsided miserably.

In a voice as cold as the Puma River waters Loren said, "You just prefer him, right? He's the big hero. Well, why should you be any different from everyone else?"

"I don't know either one of you well enough to make choices," she said, "and since I'll probably never see either one of you again, what difference does it make? But I'll tell you this, Blair would never say anything that childish, and if you're going to start pushing for choices at this stage of things, I'd have to choose him. So don't be dumb, okay? Let's just sit here and relax a while. This hasn't been one of my better days and I don't feel like hassling with anybody."

An hour later, as Loren folded his aching body into his sleeping bag, he was as near tears as he had been in a long time.

It was just too much. Everything was too much to cope with. His nerves were strained taut from the ride, and his emotions were bruised from the exhausting lifelong battle against Blair. He was without hope. It was always going to be Blair. Mom was always going to say, "Let Blair sleep. He's worn out. *You* go get what he needs."

And the Sandys were always going to say, "I've never met anyone like Blair. I choose him. Him."

And the photographers were always going to catch Blair being wonderful and Loren falling on his tail.

Well, not tomorrow, he thought grimly. This one day is going to be mine. If it kills me.

Chapter 11

"Number fourteen—go!"

Blair caught Raven as the horse tried to follow Kade. Fifteen seconds, and that's it, he thought. It's going to be today. Loren is stretching this out as long as he can, but today he'll do something. I can hear it in his voice, the way he's evading me this morning.

"Number fifteen—go! And that's it." Karen Crow's voice faded behind him as Raven surged forward. They trotted fast and straight, with no sign of a limp in Raven's gait, any faltering that would cause the judges to call them back and give Blair an honorable out.

Raven slowed a bit as Kadir's footfalls joined his own and the squeak of Loren's saddle accompanied Blair's. They rode wordlessly. After the first two miles of easy jeep trail, instead of following the dirt road they entered a single-file trail. Raven dropped behind Kade, and the two drag riders followed at a comfortable distance to the rear.

Blair tried to concentrate all his senses on the trail, to memorize it in case . . . It was much more level than yesterday's. It seemed to be rising, but only gradually. Softneedled boughs brushed his face and shoulders, on both sides. The concussions of Raven's hooves were on soft earth pungent with bruised pine needles. Although the horse moved easily under Blair, he frequently broke cadence to step carefully through or over something. Tree roots? Not rocks, there was no ring of metal shoes against rock this morning.

Compared to yesterday's gymnastics, this was an easy ride. So far. Blair's mind began to relax, to let in thoughts of Sandy. Her words came into his head, as they had come last night through the canvas tent wall.

"Blair doesn't let his blindness stop him. Gutsy guy. Never met anyone like him."

Blair's face hardened. Naturally she never met anyone like me. How many blind guys are there running around in most high schools? That's all the big attraction is, I know it and Loren knows it. My blindness is the only important thing about me. If I didn't have that, I'd be the biggest nothing in the world.

Even this fight with Loren. Whatever that's all about, it's got something to do with the blind thing. He's jealous about the newspaper story, which they wouldn't be doing about me if I was your ordinary sighted kid, and now he's probably jealous about Sandy on top of it, and who knows what all else. Damned stupid idiot, with all he's got going for him, wasting his energy trying to get back at me for whatever he thinks I've done to him, when he ought to be grabbing his advantages and running with them. Loren, you jerk.

Through the long hours of the morning Blair rode tensed and straining for whatever it was that was coming. Through the midmorning vet check, and in and out of the hour-long lunch stop, Fourteen and Fifteen remained the last riders, followed only by the two drag men.

After lunch, which was a jeepload of sandwiches and fruit juice served in what seemed to Blair to be a smallish wooded clearing, the trail began to climb more noticeably. No more branches brushed Blair, and there was steady sun now on his face. Still, the trees were there. He could smell their pine scent, and hear their whispered movement.

Were they slowing down now? Blair strained to hear other horses. He could hear neither the riders ahead of them nor the drags behind.

The sun's heat disappeared from his skin. Blair felt the scratch of a twig against his right ear and, a few minutes later, the brush of pine needles on his left thigh. Close woods again.

His horse slowed to a tentative walk.

"What's the matter?" Blair asked.

"Nothing."

Loren's voice sounded funny. Guilty? Scared?

Blair concentrated on the horse under him, and got a sense of a very slight downhill pitch and an ever-so-slight sloping off to the right, as though they might be starting a descent along a right-sloping mountainside.

He became aware of a new sound, the almost imperceptible swishing of small plants against the horse's legs and hooves.

Then he knew.

The horses stopped. Loren cleared his throat and said, "Wait a minute. I think I lost the trail. You wait here while I backtrack a little ways and see if I can find a marker."

Already Kade was crashing away through the under-brush.

Blair called, "No. Wait. I'll go with you." He tried to turn Raven but his own sudden agitation was telegraphed to the horse, and Raven stiffened and resisted. The horse spun, stepped on a rotted branch that popped under his foot and startled him into another half-spin.

Blair urged him in the direction he thought Loren and Kade had gone. Raven took one step and halted.

"Go on." Blair booted him and popped him with the ends of his reins. The horse stood rooted.

"Listen, I don't need this aggravation from you. I've got enough problems with my stupid brother."

Blair got off and tried to lead Raven forward—and walked into the broad trunk of the tree that stood in Raven's way.

He turned the horse to one side and moved to mount him, but Raven rolled his eyes and danced away. Something was wrong here. The boy was frightened. Raven could smell it on the boy's skin. And they were alone. Raven was never ridden alone. There was always another horse to follow. There was no leader here for him to trust, nobody but this boy, and if the boy was frightened, then there must be something here to be frightened of.

Raven reared suddenly, jerking the rein from Blair's hand. He whirled and bolted.

"Oh, that's just great," Blair shouted. "That's just what I need right now. Loren, you better get back here. I'm not playing this game anymore.

"I'm going to kill him," he said more quietly. Then he stopped talking to listen. The crashing sounds of Raven's flight were fading downhill and to the right.

139

"Forget him," Blair told himself. "The thing to do now is to try to get back to the main trail. That shouldn't be impossible."

First he stood without moving and tried to remember every motion, every turn that he and Raven had made together and separately. No use. There's been too much confusion.

He strained for sounds of Loren's return. There were only chattering squirrels and the occasional song of birds.

Blair lay down on his back, spreading his arms and legs to cover the maximum surface. The slope was—yes, it was downhill toward his right foot. So his head should be pointing in the general direction that they'd come.

He rolled up to kneeling position and brushed his fingers over the earth in wide arcs. Hoof prints. Lots of them, all churned around in different directions. Have to get out a ways, he decided.

Moving cautiously on his knees and hands, he left the area of churned earth and began a sideways swing to the left, brushing pine needles and small plants with his fingers, searching for a hoof-shaped depression. The ground dropped away to his left, so steeply that he knew they hadn't come that way. Feeling for his own knee-depressions, he found his way back to where he had begun the leftward swing.

To the right he crawled this time, again searching the ground with fingertips that were beginning to feel raw and oversensitive. His shoulder struck a tree trunk. He worked around it and continued.

Suddenly he stopped. There it was, a hoof-shaped depression. He leaned as far toward it as he could without

140

putting his other hand on the ground, and searched for more.

Yes! Other prints, all going the same direction, some Kade-sized, some larger.

"Loren Liskey, I'm going to get you yet," Blair muttered. He began to crawl in the direction the hoofprints came from, resting most of his weight on his left hand and feeling for prints with his right.

As he crawled, he tried to remember how long they'd ridden after they'd left the main trail. But he had no idea. His perception of the change had begun too indefinitely. His back and arms began to ache. He stood and tried walking a few steps, but then he was out of contact with the trail. It was too dangerous. That line of hoofprints was his only hope out of this mess. Wearily he dropped to his knees again and continued his inchworm progress. Crawl a step, feel, crawl a step.

He checked his watch. Two-twenty.

After a while his fingers found a new track, Kade's hooves going the same direction he was crawling. He went on.

When his back could stand the position no longer, Blair stopped to rest and to check his watch again. Ten till three.

He's not coming back for me, Blair thought bleakly. This isn't just a joke with him, he really wants to lose me up here. Maybe permanently. Does he really hate me that much? Why?

Sighing, he crawled on.

After another several minutes the ground leveled, and Blair's fingers found what he wanted. Myriads of hoofprints intersected, all going right. The main trail.

141

"Hooray," he yelled. Then, louder, "Help. Is anybody there? Help."

A chorus of his own voice echoed back from distant mountains, but when it died there was nothing, no sound but the distant kee-ing of a hawk and the rhythmic grunting of his own breath. There was no way to avoid the realization that Loren was gone, and was gone deliberately, with malice aforethought. For the first time in his life Blair felt hatred directed at him, and the sensation chilled him far more deeply than did the solitude of his situation. From early childhood he'd felt love, concern, pity, which he'd alternately loathed and used. But never hate.

He was suddenly startled to realize within himself an excitement, as though the tepid water in which he'd been paddling all his life were suddenly laced with a stream of icewater. It was shocking, bracing, and it cleared his head in such a way that he found himself focusing on Loren, struggling to put himself in the place of his fortunate, sighted younger brother.

Blair ceased to crawl and leaned back against the mountain to stretch his legs for a moment, and to ponder.

When did all this start with Lorey? It's been there all through our ride training, for sure. I knew he resented my slowing him down. I can't believe he would have wanted Sundance to bow a tendon, but he was pushing awfully hard on those hill climbs, and he did try to get me to do more cantering than was good for Dancer. I know he was hoping I'd drop out when Dance did get hurt. I'm sure Loren would have had a better chance at winning this stupid race without me, but why didn't he realize *I* needed this Trek?

The rope swings both ways, buddy.

142

Yeah. Maybe while he wasn't realizing what the Trek meant to me, *I* wasn't realizing that it meant something big to him, too. What, though? He doesn't have to prove anything to himself, like I do.

How do you know that? You've never let him see how scared you are about lots of things. Like going away to college. How do you know he's not hiding some boogeyman of his own that he doesn't want people to see?

A slow smile lit Blair's face, but he was unaware of it. For the first time in eighteen years of an existence centered solely on himself, he was managing to cross over, in his imagination, into the thoughts and feelings of someone else. Suddenly he needed to talk to Lorey, to understand completely the reasons for Loren's abandonment of him.

He stood up and tried walking along the trail. He judged it to be five or six feet wide. The uphill slope on his right was not quite steep enough for him to be able to touch it for guidance, and there seemed to be no trees nearby that might yield a branch to be used as a cane, to feel for the dropoff. Grimly Blair eased from one step to the next, seeking reassurance in the hoof-churned earth beneath his boots.

The earth grew rocky. Hoofprints disappeared. The trail curved to the right with the face of the mountain and Blair walked straight ahead.

His foot came down on air. He screamed. Gravelly earth struck his knee, hands, shoulders, face. He rolled. Something cracked him in the small of his back and the rolling ceased. A small piñon tree held him.

When he could breathe again and move his trembling limbs, Blair crawled up, up and over the lip of the trail. He lay there for several minutes pumping oxygen into his

143

lungs. His fright began to wash away and beneath it lay a nugget of realization.

I've gone through the worst. I've survived it.

He laughed out loud. Then he began to crawl again.

Loren reined Kadir to a halt. He'd been making good time since he got back on the trail and now, through the trees ahead, he caught a flash of the pale chaps of the drag riders. Plan B, he thought. Now or never. He eased Kade into a slow jog and rehearsed it again.

When he caught up to the drags he'd say, "Gee, I thought you guys were behind us. We got off the trail back there a ways for a bathroom break, you guys must have passed us then and we didn't know it. Listen, would you go back and get my brother? His horse was giving out, so he told me to go ahead, he'd ride in with you. We thought you were right behind us."

Did it sound believable?

Yes.

But what about Blair? What was he going to say to the drags, to Mom and Dad? That was the weak part of Plan B. There might be hell to pay, Loren thought grimly, but at least I'll have gotten far enough ahead of him that I'll still be in the running for the trophy. Once Blair and the drags get together, he'll just finish out the ride with them. He'll be fine. He doesn't really need me, just any other rider, that's all he needs. And Kade and I—

A sound came faintly through the crystal air. A scream? Blair? No, it wouldn't have been.

But . . .

He halted Kade and turned to watch the trail behind him. He could see stretches of it wrapping around the mountainside for some distance behind him. Raven should be appearing somewhere along there, he thought. He hesitated and stared at the trail while precious racing time ticked past.

The mountain was still. Ahead of Loren, the drag riders vanished. Behind him somewhere was his brother, and a sound that might have been a call for help. Or a bird or wild animal. Probably that.

"I've got to get going," he told himself frantically. "I'm losing time. I've already lost too much. I can't go back for Blair."

But the stillness around him echoed with accusation.

He laid his rein against Kadir's neck and moved the horse out at a hard trot, back along the trail, away from the junior division trophy.

With every stride of Kade's legs Loren's guilt pressed more heavily, until his very breathing became a battle. All of the small rotten things he'd done to Blair during the course of their boyhoods began to gather in his mind, to snowball into this one overwhelming and unforgivable act.

God, no wonder people like Blair better than me.

As he rode, a determination crystalized in Loren's mind. No matter how this Trek turned out, no matter if either of them finished the thing, and no matter what Blair told people about what Loren had done to him, Loren was going to hash this thing out with Blair, apologize, of course, but really try to make him understand all the complicated whys behind the betrayal.

With that resolve made, Loren turned his attention to the business at hand. It was odd that Raven was still out of sight, he thought. They should have been closer behind me than this.

Loren tried not to look to his right, where the ground disappeared. It wasn't a completely sheer drop; it had enough slope to hold trees and outcroppings of rock, but it was steep enough to make his stomach uneasy. The trail at this point snaked around a series of blind curves that followed the undulating face of the mountain. Around each curve Loren expected to see Raven and Blair.

His uneasiness grew until it outweighed caution, and he put Kade in a canter. They started around a tight curve that circled a jutting rock formation.

Suddenly a creature appeared, startlingly low, just under Kade's nose. A blur of white moved upward.

Loren yelped in surprise. Kade reared, plunged to the right, stumbled as his forefeet dropped off the rim of the trail and sank into loose scree. He went to his knees.

Loren grabbed for the saddle horn and missed, somersaulted over Kade's shoulders. The horse, pulled off balance by the reins Loren still clutched, snaked his head toward the sky and rolled downward.

Through the tumbling flashes of sky, earth, trees, rocks, Loren saw the mass of brown coming down on top of him. He had time only to scream.

Chapter 12

For a few moments Blair lay sprawled across the trail, stunned from the glancing blow of Kade's front hoof. When he came to, he was unaware of the blood oozing steadily down his neck.

"Loren?" His voice was so shaky he could barely hear it himself through the ringing in his ears. He tried again. "Loren? Are you okay?"

No voice answered, but he thought he heard ragged breathing.

Cautiously he crept forward until his hand found the edge of the dropoff. Loose, freshly dug chunks of soil met his fingers at the place where Kade's hooves had plowed over the edge and into the loose scree below it.

Blair stretched his arm down, testing the pitch of the slope. Then, without allowing himself time to think about it, he swung his legs down and began a sliding, feet-first descent.

It was his foot that first felt the soft give of Loren's leg. Instantly Blair reached for him.

"Loren?"

In a rage of helplessness Blair felt his brother's face,

traced the position of his body and limbs. No sound came from Loren, but the ribcage rose and fell in shallow breaths. For a mad instant Blair pictured himself taking Loren's PRs. He made a sound that was laugh and sob and gagging combined.

Softly Loren moaned.

Blair put his face close to Loren's and said, "It's me. Blair. Can you hear me?"

Loren made no sound, but his fingers found and locked on the cuff of Blair's jeans.

"Listen, Lor. I have to go back up to the trail and leave something up there. My shirt, or something, so they can see it when they come looking for us. They'll be coming pretty soon. Can you hear me? I have to leave for just a minute, but I'll be right back."

"No. Stay." The words were barely audible.

"I'll be right back. I have to." Blair loosened the fingers that held his jeans, and began the upward climb. He concentrated on going straight up the hill, and on estimating the distance. At the place where the slope leveled to support the trail, he took off his tee shirt and spread it across the dirt, then slid back down to Loren.

"I'm back," he said softly, but there was no answer, only the shallow breath-sounds. From somewhere downhill and to the right came the sound of movement through grass, and the creak of an empty saddle.

Blair arranged his long body in a protective curve around Loren, and settled in to wait.

By a stream bank three miles away, the drag riders stopped their horses and dismounted beside two PR girls and the team of judges.

Dr. Ruden said, "Where are Fourteen and Fifteen? The Liskey boys."

John Marshall looked at his partner, Dave, and together they shrugged their shoulders. "They were right ahead of us. They didn't check through yet?"

Both PR girls and both judges rechecked their clipboards. "No, Fourteen and Fifteen definitely haven't come through."

John and Dave remounted.

Dr. Ruden started toward the jeep that stood near the stream. "You guys start back. I'll get on the radio and get some help back here, just in case. They probably just wandered off the trail somewhere, but we better not take any chances. Can I get through there with the jeep, do you think?"

John shook his head. "Too narrow. We'll give you the word when we find them," he patted the two-way radio clipped to his belt, "and if we need help, somebody will have to horseback in there after us."

Blair came to a fuzzy state of semiwakefulness. He heard someone say, "The little guy needs a stretcher for sure, and this one looks pretty shocky to me. I think we'll have to carry them both out."

He tried to tell them he was all right, but his mouth didn't work. He was floating up the hill. From beyond his feet came the voice of one of the PR girls.

From a distance he heard his own voice saying, "Are my readings okay?"

But she was straining to carry her end of the stretcher up a steep mountainside on tricky footing. She had no wind left for talking.

*   *   *

Blair woke when the morning sun touched his face and brightened his area of vision. Cautiously he sat up and pushed back the light hospital blanket. His head hurt, and his hands and knees and most of the muscles in his body, but beneath the surface aches he felt the buoyancy of a survivor. An achiever.

From the bed next to him Loren said, "Hey, hermano, how you doing?" The voice was somewhat weak but stronger than it had been last night. Blair got out of his bed and felt his way to Loren's.

"Will it joggle you if I sit here?"

"No, go ahead. Ouch. No, that's okay."

They both talked in subdued voices, aware of the sleeping man in the room's third bed.

Loren said, "My memory's a little fuzzy about last night. They set my leg or something, didn't they?"

"Greenstick fracture of your left leg," Blair recited, "broken collarbone, slight concussion, but nothing to be worried about. A nice variety of cuts and bruises."

"That's what I thought. You're okay, though?"

"Sure. Couple of stitches over my ear, from Kade's foot. Mainly they just wanted me to stay overnight for observation. And I wanted to, anyway, to keep you company."

Silence. Blair felt Loren gathering himself to say something difficult. Embarrassed, he turned the conversation. "The horses are fine. You were getting your leg set last night when Karen Crow was here, and you were so dopey after that, there wasn't any time to tell you. But I figured you'd be worried about Kade."

"Yeah," Loren breathed.

"His knees got cut up some, but they led him out okay,

150

and Mom said Dr. Ruden gave him a good going over when they got back to camp and he says he'll be fine."

"What about Raven? What happened, Blair? How come you were crawling along the trail?"

"He got away from me back where . . . we first got off the main trail. I got off him to try to figure out which way to go, and he spooked and got away from me. I guess the lunch crew spotted him and got hold of him. He broke a rein, that was all."

"Lucky."

"Yeah."

The silence grew as Loren struggled for a way to start what he had to say.

Blair said, "I'll tell you one thing, baby brother, if we decide to do the Trek again next summer, I'm riding Sundance or I'm not going. If we start conditioning the horses earlier in the spring so we don't have to push so hard, and get him muscled up more gradually . . ."

"Next year?" Loren's voice broke.

"Sure. Why not?"

"You'd trust me?" Loren whispered.

Blair shifted uncomfortably. "Hey, look. You did a rotten thing, I know that, you know that. I'm not sure I understand why, but one of these days if you want to talk about it, we will, okay? But in the meantime, it's not that big a deal. Listen, being me isn't easy sometimes, but being my brother probably isn't always beer and skittles, either, so let's just leave it at that, okay buddy?"

"Just one thing," Loren said.

"What's that?"

"What the hell is a skittle?"

Their laughter woke the man in the other bed.